Nolan

BENTLEY LEGACY Book 3

KATHI S. BARTON

World Castle Publishing, LLC
Pensacola, Florida
Copyright © Kathi S. Barton 2015
Hardback ISBN: 9781629893648
Paperback ISBN: 9781629893655
eBook ISBN: 9781629893662
First Edition World Castle Publishing, LLC, December 14, 2015
http://www.worldcastlepublishing.com
Licensing Notes
Cover: Karen Fuller
Editor: Eric Johnston
Editor: Maxine Bringenberg

Chapter 1

Nolan looked around his new office. He'd never had one of his own before. The other practice that he'd been working for had a community one they'd all shared...several doctors using the same computer in the same small ten-by-ten room. This was his and his alone. Burke, too, would have his own office when his notice was up at the hospital. For now he was working just a couple of hours a week to help Nolan out. And his office was going to wait, he told Nolan, until he could really devote his time to it.

The walls were decorated with just Nolan's things. It was a small thing to be happy about, he supposed. His diplomas were there, along with his awards...and there were plenty of those, as he'd always been a hard worker. Plus, he'd been able to bring in pictures of his family...his mom and grandparents. The photo of his father in his uniform about a month before he'd been killed had a prominent place on his wall, along with some of the things that he treasured above all else, such as smaller pictures of just him and his father. And his brothers too, the ones that were currently pissed at him.

He supposed if he was honest with himself, he was the one that was pissed. He'd needed their help, yes, and their support on the project that he'd been trying to get up off the ground for months now. Nolan knew that he'd of gotten it there, but the fact was he was too broke to go on and would have lost it all if they hadn't sat him down and told him they were going to help him, in any way they could.

"But I can do this." Even Garth, the money maker in the family, shook his head. "You just don't understand. This is something that I want to do, and I don't want you taking over."

His mom, the best mom in the entire world, had given him the most disappointed look he'd ever seen. His heart broke then, and that had made his temper lash out at the entire family. But his pride had won out on making things up to his mom.

"Fine. Go ahead and take over. Like you do everything else. It wouldn't be the Bentley clan thing if you guys didn't have your two cents in it too, now would it? And that's what bothered you so much." He started to get up and leave them to their "intervention," but his mother stood up and ordered him to sit. "I'm not ten. You can't treat me this way."

"You are my son and I will treat you how you act. Sit down." He sat, but he'd been a little more than pissed. Holding his temper had always served him well, but right now he wasn't trying all that hard. "How much money have you spent on this amazing project?"

"Everything." There was no point in lying to them. They all knew, he was sure. "But it was worth every penny, and I'm going to put more into it when I have it."

"Good." Her answer surprised him. "You think that I'm not proud of what you've done? Do you think...well you do, don't you? You've proven that, haven't you? Do you think that any of us would want you to not be able to make this dream of yours work? That we'd just let you fail at something that you've worked so hard at?"

"I don't want your help. I can do this on my own." His mother only sat down and pushed an envelope at him. "I'm not taking your money, Mom. It's what we all worked for so that you'd be set for the rest of your life."

"I am set. I have my sons here. And their families. And this isn't only from me. We all put money in here." The envelope was pushed at him until it was right at his fingertips. "Take it or not. It's entirely up to you. But if you fail at this—and you will, because you're not letting us help you when you need it—then I do not want to hear a single word from you. And your father's name on this place will be a terrible legacy to him should you not let your family support you as he did us."

She'd gotten up and moved to the door, her last sentence stinging him the hardest. When they'd all left him, even his two nieces, he sat there for ten more minutes before he got up and snatched the envelope up before going to his car. He'd not been back home since.

"Doctor Nolan?" Nolan looked up at Loraine Bean, the nurse that had worked for him at his old practice and had begged to come and work for him here. "There's a patient here that needs some attention. He didn't have an appointment, and I can't get anything from him. I think he's been hurt pretty badly."

Nolan stood up and told her to take him to the examining room, that he'd be right there. She nodded but didn't move.

"I don't think...he's just a kid, not much bigger than my own son. About thirteen or so. He won't even tell me his name." Nolan paused in pulling on his lab coat to ask her what the boy had said to her. "Nothing other than to show me his arm, and I came to get you."

"Show him in and I'll be there in a moment." She nodded again and left. He wasn't sure what was going on, but he would help the child. Going down the hall, he tried to think what would have happened, and realized he was probably making it a great deal worse than it was.

Entering the room, he looked at his patient. The kid turned to him, and two things struck Nolan at once. The kid was afraid of him, and he was human. The scent of blood, strong and fresh, made Nolan's cat make himself known. Nolan decided to go slowly.

"My name is Nolan Bentley. I'm the doctor who is going to look at you." The kid nodded, and Nolan sat on the stool while the kid sat on the big exam table. "What is it you're here to see me about?"

The kid peeled the dishtowel from his forearm. Nolan could see that it had been bleeding a great deal. The towel, like his sleeve, was soaked through, and he was wincing as the skin was exposed. Someone had cut him, badly and deeply.

"Can you tell me what happened?" The boy said nothing, but stared at him. "I can't help you unless you help me. If you were cut by a fence or something like that, you'd need to have a tetanus shot first. Then I'd have to make sure there was no rust or anything in the cut. If it was a knife, I'd have to know what sort of knife. Were you cutting chicken and the blade slipped? Maybe you got hit by a piece of falling glass. Or you —"

"Knife. A switchblade." Nolan nodded and pulled on some gloves. "I'm…he tried to take my money. Not that I have much, but I worked for it. He's bigger, so it's not like I didn't try to protect myself, but…he's bigger."

"I don't blame you." Nolan rolled a table with all the things he'd need to stitch him up toward them and had the kid put his arm over it so he could look at it better. "It's going to need about twenty-five or so stitches. But it will need to be cleaned out first. What does the other kid look like? The one that hurt you. Other than big, I mean. Did you get some good licks in yourself?"

"He just left me there. I don't think he's hurting though. He's a known bully and has a gang that hangs with him. I might have hit him a few times, but it was just luck, not anything more." Nolan told him what he was going to do, and the kid just watched. Opening the wound up, he could see that while it was very deep, it had cut no major veins or tendons. But it was going to be sore for a while.

"Do you have a parent or guardian you can have my nurse call?" When the boy didn't answer him, Nolan stopped looking at the wound and looked at him. "I have to make a call to her or the police. If she's the one that did this to you, then I can get you some —"

"No. She'd never do that…it's not her. It's the man that thinks he can boss her around a lot that I worry about." Nolan frowned, wondering what sort of life this kid had. "He's a real douche canoe. And no matter how many times she tells him to back off, he's right up in our face. And she's not my mom, but my aunt."

"All right. We'll still have to call her. This guy, does he live with you two?" The kid shook his head hard. "Then I don't understand how it's going to be an issue with her being called."

"They took the car last week because money is so short. We knew they were going to. It's been hard on us since my mom passed away a few months ago." Nolan felt his heart break for the kid. "Aunt Rylee has been working hard, but not having a car, she won't be able to get here now. Plus, the buses don't run that late on her second job. Walking home at night is dangerous, but she is trying really hard."

"And what is your name? For the records. And if you give me her address, I can have someone go and pick her up and bring her here." The kid was shaking his head. "No one will hurt her or you now that you're here. I swear that to you."

"I know that. But she's...she's not very...she's been under a lot of stress. And she freaks out really easy. Not badly, but...last night she cried for two hours because she didn't have the money for me to go on this class thing. I told her it was okay, but she is...she's weird about that sort of stuff. She's this really...she was in the army when Mom called her, and she was so...Mom said it was army life, but she was so hard. But now she's sort of...I guess squishy. Cries about stuff that's okay, and then gets all blown up when things are an injustice, as she calls them. I really love her, but she's weird, like I said."

"I see. Let me get her address and I'll have my mom go and get her. She's understanding about this sort of thing." The kid still didn't seem convinced, and Nolan had to admire him for protecting his family. "She's going to have to find out sooner or later, I'm afraid. You can't just hide something like this from her. She'll be more hurt if you do, I bet. My mom would be."

"All right, but don't say that I didn't warn you. Her name is really Rylee McClure." He also gave him the address. "My name is Shane. Shane Cole."

The phone in the examining room was there for him to use, but for the life of him he had no idea how to contact his mother on it. She had a cell phone, he supposed, but whenever he needed her he would just reach out to contact her through their link. He did that now.

I need your cell number. She laughed and gave it to him. *Okay. I need to call you. Will you be able to answer me?*

Yes. I'm assuming this is for someone else's benefit? He told her it was and why. *I see. Go ahead and call me then. I'm with Reggie and Chris. The three of us were going to go to the grocery, but this will be fun too.*

He called her and explained again what he needed. Giving her both their names and the address, he could hear his sister-in-law in the background laughing. Reggie was talking to one of the babies, he knew from the sound of her voice, and was telling them how Uncle Nolan was a doctor woctor. Whatever the hell that meant. Hanging up a few minutes later, he sat back down on the chair and started cleaning the wound out while talking with young Shane.

~~~

The doorbell nearly scared ten years off her life. Rylee had had her head in the dryer, trying to find the last sock that had been there when she'd put it in the stupid thing, but now was missing. She not only bumped her head, but was pretty sure that the sock was eaten, again by the stupid machine. She was still rubbing her head when she went to the door and peeked out the side glass.

It wasn't Mike, thank goodness. But whatever the two women were selling, she had no money for, nor did she have time for their spiel. Opening the door, she could see

Mike coming out of his townhouse next door and staring at them like he wasn't going anywhere until he had all the information she did. The nosey prick was driving her nuts. Just as the elder woman opened her mouth to speak, Mike cut her off.

"You said you weren't going to be home tonight. You never told me about no company." She ignored him for the two women. "I don't think you should be letting them in. They look shifty to me. And if you got no plans, then you can go with me to the movies like I told you we could. That boy of yours, he can stay home. I don't like him either."

Her temper nearly got the better of her. Rylee hated Mike Packer and wanted to murder him daily, but lately, since her sister had died, he'd been making a total ass of himself, bugging her and telling her what she should and shouldn't be doing. And when her car had gotten repossessed, he'd been all over that like white on rice. He insisted that he be the one to drive her all over town, going so far as to send cabs that she'd call for away when they arrived at her house.

The younger woman spoke before she could. "Fuck off, buddy. We're not here to see you, so go the fuck back in your house." Well, that took religious zealots off the list of who they might be, Rylee thought with a grin. The older woman tisked at the younger one, who did not look the least bit repentant when she said she was sorry. Mike made his way back into his house, but his door, forever opening and closing like a damned revolving door lately, stood open just a little.

"Are you Rylee McClure?" Rylee told her she was, a finger of fear going down her back. "I'm sorry, my dear, do you think we could go inside? Your neighbor seems to think this has something to do with him."

Mike's door slammed shut and the older woman smiled at her. For reasons she could not understand, she liked them both. And when she invited them in, she knew that she'd be as safe with them as she would with her gun pointed to whoever might be coming for her. A strange thought, but lately a lot of things had been strange.

"Do you have a child...nephew...by the name of Shane...I don't remember what Nolan told us his last name was, do you, Chris?" She told her. "Yes, that's right. Shane Cole. Do you know him?"

Her vision began to blur and her heart...she actually looked down at her chest to see if it had fallen out of her chest. She could not lose him too. He was all she had in the world now that...when the room began to tilt, she heard the younger women cursing and thought perhaps she'd like to learn a few of those words soon. Before she knew it, she was on the floor with her head between her upright knees.

"Just breathe, young lady. It's not that bad. Or so he said." Rylee asked her who. "My son. He's a doctor. A very good one. And your nephew came to his office a little while ago and had to be looked at. I don't know a great many of the details, but I do know that if anyone can keep him safe, it will be my son." Rylee wondered if she thought this was helping, because it wasn't.

"Gracie, you're not helping her. She's scared to death that he's hurt really badly." Gracie, the older woman, Rylee assumed, asked her to talk to Nolan and find out. "I have a better idea. Why don't we just take her to him? Like he wanted us to. She might feel better to see him even if we were to tell her he's just fine."

"Oh. Yes. That's a good idea. I think the man next door...did you smell him?" Chris must have answered because Gracie continued as if she had. "And what was he wearing? No man should be out looking like…well, he just rolled out of the barn after mucking it all day."

Rylee laughed. As she pushed gently against the hand holding her down, she was freed. Looking up from her position on the floor, she smiled at the two of them. Then the door opened again and a woman holding two babies came in too. One of them was screaming her head off.

"Here." A baby was handed to Chris, and then the screaming one was shoved in her arms. "Where is your bathroom? I have to go now. I thought you said you'd only be…where?"

Rylee told her down the hall, but kept her eyes on the little girl in her arms. Christ, she was beautiful, and the way her little lips puckered up like she was going to let go of another healthy scream made Rylee's heart melt.

"Hey there, little one. Don't cry. Mommy will be back in a second." The little girl just stared at her. Her cheeks looked so downy soft that Rylee had to touch them. Adjusting her in her hands, she ran her finger down her cheek and marveled at not just the softness of it, but also how warm she was.

"Her name is Alexis. And this is Anna. They're my granddaughters." Rylee looked at the baby that was now in Gracie's hands and could see that they were twins. "She likes you."

"I never held a baby this tiny before. When Shane was born, I was away and…. Oh my God, Shane. Can you take me to him?" The baby started to cry again but hushed once Rylee started talking to the adults again in a calm and quiet voice. "I don't have a car anymore. And if I call a cab, I think that Mike will intercept it again and I'll end up in his car. I'll give you some gas money. I don't…well, not a lot of gas money, but I managed to find ten dollars in the dryer today. I was going to take Shane out for a treat, but...." She closed her mouth when she realized she was babbling. Not a habit she'd developed until recently. Gracie just smiled at her and stood up.

"We were actually sent to get you." Handing the baby back to her mom when she returned, Rylee asked for a minute to get something on. She ran to her bedroom and changed in record time, and put on her jacket as she made her way to the living room again. When Gracie asked her if she was set, they left with Rylee making sure the doors were locked three times before she walked down the sidewalk.

"You need a safer place to stay." She looked over at Chris, who was sitting in the front with Gracie as she drove. "That man next door, he's going to hurt you if you don't."

"I don't think he'll hurt me now. A couple of weeks ago he tried that crap on me and I put him in his place. He had been backing off until today. I think he might need another show of force." Gracie laughed, but Chris didn't look convinced. "He's harmless for the most part. And when he gets out of line, I put him back in his place. I have...I can carry and I do now. I don't care for it, but I have to protect us."

She asked what they knew about Shane. Chris answered her, but Rylee had a feeling that she was still worried about the neighbor. He really wasn't that bad, but she knew how to handle him when he was.

"Nolan said that he's been cut on his arm with a knife. I don't know the extent of the wound other than without someone there that can authorize him to work on it, he has to wait. Shane told him that you no longer had a car." She waited for someone to tell her she should work harder to keep her things, but none of them said a word about that as Chris continued. "He isn't much of a talker, is he?"

"No." Rylee wanted to tell them that was her fault too. He'd been so depressed since his mom had died, but she was having so much trouble shaking her own depression about Shelby dying that it was hard for her to talk to him about his own. She also knew that there had been some trouble at school, but again, he'd not shared much in the way of information, only to tell her that he had it handled. Obviously not.

As they drove her to the nicer part of town, she realized that they knew her name, but other than first names, she had no idea who they were. She started to ask them when the car turned into a nice office building parking lot and the engine was turned off. They all turned to her.

"I'm a little scared." Gracie told her that was understandable. "I'm not...it's been hard on us. For the last few months, it's been really hard on us. We can't seem to get a break. To be telling you this...sharing...I'm not sure why I feel I can, but I've not had a great deal of friends over, and those that do come over are more interested in why we're so broke. I really hate people."

"Not all people are like your so-called friends. And so you know, we trust you as well. But you need help. We can help you." Rylee shook her head at Chris as she nodded. "We can and we will. You will need us as much as we do you. Go inside and we'll be in soon. Nolan is on the phone right now with his brother about something, and Shane is with the nurse. Nolan will help you too...he'll need to. His nurse is waiting on you to fill out the paperwork."

The sharp intake of breath from Gracie had Rylee looking at her. But she was staring at Chris, smiling. There was something there, something that she felt like she needed to know but wasn't sure she actually wanted to know it. Before they could tell her that something else had happened, she got out of the car and made her way to the front door alone. The nurse was standing at the door like she'd been waiting on her and let her in.

"Hello, I'm Nurse Loraine Bean. Your nephew is in the office right now. I've given him something to settle his stomach…nothing more than a little soda. Nolan Bentley, the doctor, is on the phone." Rylee nodded. "Can you please fill out this paperwork? All it's staying is that you give him permission to put stitches in his arm."

"Can I see him first? I'd feel so much better if you'd let me just make sure that it's him. I know it is, but I have to see him." The nurse smiled and nodded. "Thank you."

"No problem. He's a good boy once he starts to talk to you. It took Nolan a little bit to get him to open up. I think they've been talking manly things, because when I come into the room, they quiet up again." The room where she was taking her had the door closed. "As I said, Nolan had to step out for a moment. But you should just go on in and talk to Shane to help him relax. Then we can get the paperwork finished up. Nolan can work on him when he gets back."

Nodding and taking a deep breath, Rylee opened the door and moved into the room. Shane was sitting there with his head leaning against the wall and his arm wrapped up in a gauze-like material. There was a kit nearby him. She was sure it was the sterile dressing and equipment used to work on him, so she was careful not to touch it. He started sobbing as soon as he saw her.

"I'm so sorry they had to come and get you like that." She told him it was fine. "I thought I could take care of it on my own, but I messed up. He had a knife and I didn't. Not that I'd use one, but Nolan said I'd need to learn how or I'd just cut myself more. And he cut me up before I could even think that was what he was going to do…the boy did, not Nolan. I'm really sorry, Aunt Rylee."

"Oh, honey, it's all right. I'm just glad that you're all right. But who did this? This kid that's been giving you problems, he took a knife to school?" He nodded, still crying. "You should have told me, Shane. We'll work this out. The doctor, is he taking care of you all right? He's not hurt you?"

"No. He's really cool. He never told me I was stupid for taking him on when I did. Said that I should have told you so you could have done something smarter. I like him." Rylee nodded and hugged him again. "Aunt Rylee, I know we don't have the money for this and I told him that. He said that I was his practice patient."

"Practice? How long as he been a doctor? Surely he's not just out of med school?" The door opened just as she asked, and she turned to see a very tall, extremely handsome man in a lab coat come in the room. "You're the doctor?"

"Yes, but not Nolan. He had to leave. I'm his brother, Burke. I'm a doctor too, as a matter of fact. And we've both been at it for some time, I assure you." She felt her face heat up, but she sat on the edge of the bed near Shane when he asked her to. "Nolan said that you've been cut with a switchblade?"

"Yes. This older boy at the school, he said that he wanted my money, and since I don't have a lot, he got a lot of blood on him for nothing. And I think I might have hurt him a little too." She was surprised to hear the man say good, but before she could say anything to him, Shane continued. "Nolan said that I should have told my aunt the truth from the start and it might not have gotten this far."

"More than likely not. When my brothers and I fight, we are usually pretty rough about it. One time when my brother Micah and I had this huge fight, my mom hosed us down with the kitchen sink thing. It sure made us pay attention when she told us to take it outside next time." Shane laughed, and Rylee could see the woman she'd met doing something like that. "Okay, young man. How about we get you put back together? Ms. Cole, you can stay or not, but the nurse is going to give him something to relax him a bit."

As soon as she nodded to Shane that it was okay, the nurse wiped a swab over his arm and stuck him. In minutes, he was closing his eyes and was asleep in no time. She looked at the doctor, worried, when he stood up. She stood as well.

"Nolan seems to think there is more to this than a cut arm. He asked me to have a look when you got here so that...he didn't want you to think that we had done this to him when he came in this way. I assure you, we'd never harm him. May I?" Nodding again, she moved back out of his way when he stood over her nephew and watched the doctor lift Shane's shirt up. "Just as he said it might be. I'm afraid he's going to need more than some stitches, Ms. Cole. He's going to need the hospital."

She could only stare at the bruising on his ribs and the blood from several other cuts that seemed to stretch up to his throat and shoulders. When Burke pulled up Shane's pant legs too, she could see where he'd been kicked, his legs scraped and bruised a great deal. Sitting down again, she had started to cry when someone was suddenly holding her. Sobbing into the shoulder of Mrs. Bentley was the best thing that had happened to her in months. Being held like this made her cry harder.

Chapter 2

"You were right on all of it...about Shane, I mean. Someone beat the shit out of him, and they did it over a long period, too. I'd say it's been going on for a few weeks if not longer. How did you know?" Nolan looked over Shane's chart and then looked up at his brother, Burke. "Did he say anything?"

"No, he didn't say anything to me. I'm not even sure he would have mentioned the cut on his arm had it not been bleeding so much. But his breathing was off, and he moved oddly when he thought no one was looking. I know that's a stupid thing to say, but I had a feeling that he'd been fighting this kid for a while now, like you said, taking his money and all. And I doubted that he'd just cut him. When did the other kid show up at our offices?" Burke nodded as if he understood. "Shane said he might have gotten in a few licks, but nothing like had happened to him."

"He showed up yesterday about four. About the time Shane showed up. But if Shane only hit him a couple of times, then the kid has an enemy in someone else. Black eye, busted lip. And he's being treated for a couple of broken ribs as well. Nasty cut on his neck, too, that looks to me like a belt or a whip had hit him. A few times too." Nolan wondered if the kid was being beaten at home. He had no idea why that occurred to him, but he'd bet anything that the apple didn't fall far from the tree. "His parents are having a fit that the cops are not letting them in to see him until he's been examined. They're claiming that he plays football and that's how he got hurt. I'm pretty sure I was never hurt that way when I played ball. How about you?"

"The only time I got hurt in a game was when you tripped me up going into the showers. I think you busted my lip and bruised up some ribs. Do you believe him?" Burke just snorted. "I have to talk to Shane's aunt. I'm thinking she'll need to press charges on this kid, or Shane's life will never be any better at that school. I'm not sure if that'll help or not, but it might get him to back off."

"Mom talked to her before Shane was brought in. They've been having some major issues at home. Not anything domestic, but just money. Rylee was in the army until a year ago. When her sister got sick, she left there to come home and care for her. From what I've been able to find out, they'd take her back in a heartbeat. She's something of a hard ass. Wouldn't have thought that to see her yesterday, but stress can do that to someone." Nolan nodded. He knew a great deal about stress. "Are you doing better?"

"I guess. I had to go and see to some things that came up yesterday at the shelter, so thanks for covering for me. I think...there are questions that need answers that I have none for. Did you know that Mom is running a charity thing there the night before we open the doors?" Burke nodded. "Why didn't anyone mention it to me?"

Instead of answering him, Burke reached over the desk at the nurse's station and handed him a sheet of paper. It was about the event and what it was going to help. Looking around, he could see them plastered all over the place now, and thought maybe he'd seen a couple of billboards around town as well. He just laid the paper down and tried to control his temper.

"Nolan. This is a good thing you're doing. But there was no reason whatsoever for you to lose it all to make it happen. We are more than glad to help you. And no one has taken over one thing that you didn't ask us to help you with." Nolan picked up the paper and showed it to Burke. "She asked you about it. You told her to do whatever she wanted. I think you hurt her with your answer, as a matter of fact. And she's been trying for a few days now to get you to tell her she's done a good thing helping."

"I'm done working on this. It's...I know I've said this before, but I wanted this to be my project. I feel that it's not that anymore." His brother just laughed. "This isn't funny, Burke. I worked hard on making this happen. And now that you all have stepped in, I feel like I've lost something."

"Yes, you did. You lost your ability to be generous and nice. And since we all have been helping you, you've just given up on it. Why is that? You have your panties in a twist about this, and you thought that since it couldn't be the great Nolan Bentley's last stand that you'd just sit with your thumb up your ass and let everyone else do the work? Mom has done nothing but try for weeks to get you involved again. Grandda is about ready to kick your ass, and Grandma is hurt that you won't even return her calls when she's gone to you about decorations." Nolan flushed.

He had been avoiding them about anything to do with the shelter, or anything else, for days now. "And you should know that Shane is looking to speak to you. He said that he wanted to have a man-to-man conversation with you."

"Great. He more than likely wants a piece of me as well." The hit to the back of his head hurt, but he didn't even bother saying anything to Burke. He'd get him later.

Going down the hall to Shane's room, he glanced at the chart in his hand again before entering. He was going to release him soon. Maybe tomorrow. There were no complications with his beat-up body, but he wanted to make sure that there was no infection in his arm before he let him go. Shane really had taken a beating.

The kid was laying on the bed with the remote to the television in his hand. A glance to the set on the wall told him that it was off. Instead of commenting on it, he just cleared his throat and moved deeper into the room. That's when he saw the woman.

She was asleep, her body curled up in a tight ball that he knew would make him sore if he tried it. He knew she was tall — just looking at her long legs gave him that hint — but it was her face, relaxed in slumber, that kept him staring.

She was beautiful. No, that wasn't right, she was more than that. But what mesmerized him were the dark circles that were so ingrained into her cheeks that they looked to be permanent. Her lips were full, and naked from any kind of makeup. Her face, the freckles on her nose made him think that she enjoyed the outdoors as much as he did. When someone spoke to his left, he turned to look at Shane, who was grinning at him.

"She's exhausted, I guess. Aunt Rylee has been working a couple of jobs or more for about three months now. We're not going to be able to afford this either." Moving to the bed instead of the woman, Nolan sat in the other chair in the room and spoke to Shane as quietly as he could.

"You won't have to worry about this. I've got an in with the hospital." Shane said she'd not like that any better than owing the hospital. "Yeah, I think I might have figured that out after she spoke to my nurse yesterday."

Shane's grin had him smiling back. "She's got a nasty temper on her. Mom used to say she could cut you to ribbons with her tongue and never even raise her voice. And her men were terrified of her."

"I heard she was in the service. It was good of her to come home to help out when you needed her. That's what family does, I know, but they can be a bit overbearing too." Shane nodded and looked over at her. Nolan did the same. "She's very beautiful, isn't she?"

"She won't think very highly of you if you point that out. Said that looks don't even come into what a person is. I think she's nuts. But that's only me." Nolan looked at the boy now and wondered at the sadness in his voice. "She didn't have to take me in, you know? When Mom found out she only had a little while to live, calling her was way down on her list. She said that Aunt Rylee had a good life and there was no reason to make her worry over nothing. Aunt Rylee was really mad when Mom told her that."

"I bet." He pulled out the notes that the officer had given him yesterday when he'd taken pictures of Shane's injuries. "I have to talk to you about the kid that cut you up. He is saying that—"

"Who the fuck are you? And what the fuck are you doing in our room?" Nolan stood up when Rylee spoke. He'd been wrong about her being tall. She was Amazon tall, and more beautiful than any woman he'd ever seen before now that she was spitting angry. "Well?"

"I'm Nolan Bentley. I was the doctor that saw your nephew—"

"No, you're not. You look like him, but you're not him. I'm tired but not that tired. What do you mean, questioning him without my permission? I'm his guardian, and I won't have you badgering him—"

"What the hell is wrong with you?" She took a step back at his temper. "I've been a doctor at this hospital for a good long time, and no one has questioned my ability to do my job. I'm asking him about his injuries. Which, in the event you didn't notice, were given to him by someone that has been beating the shit out of him for months now." Nolan knew that he was blowing this way out of right field, but he, too, was tired and his temper not the best of things lately. "Sit down and behave if you think you can. I have a patient here and he needs my attention."

She looked hurt, shocked, and out of sorts. He had to hand it to her...she could bring her temper down quicker than he could. But when she sat down and leaned back in the chair, he knew that she was beaten, and his heart ached for her.

"I didn't know." Her entire body sagged at her confession. "He said he had it handled. And I thought he did. It's my fault he's beaten up like this. I should have...I'm not any good at this parenting thing."

Nolan reached for her just as Shane moved on the bed. He wasn't sure what the kid could do, banged up the way that he was, but as soon as Nolan touched her, he knew what she was to him. Her body, warm and strong, leaned into his even as he buried his nose into her neck. Christ, his body screamed at him, she was his. Licking her throat, tasting her, he could hear her moan, but when his head was jerked up by his hair, all he could do was stare at her.

Her cheeks were wet with tears, but the fury in her eyes made him think that he was going to die right then and there. He wondered briefly if he kissed her, would that be enough to take him on to the next life, if there was one, or would he always wonder?

"What are you doing?" He heard her, even though her voice was low and her body had not moved from his. "Did you just…taste me?"

"Yes. And I'd very much like to do more." Her hand yanked harder on his hair and he couldn't help it, he rocked into her folds as he cupped her ass. "I never thought I'd find you. And here you are."

"Aunt Rylee?" Nolan groaned, having forgotten all about the young man that was on the bed. "What's going on? Are you okay? I don't think you should kill the doctor. I don't know what would happen to me if you did, and there is the point that he said he could make this bill go away too."

Rylee looked at her nephew, who nodded, then back at him. Nolan could see that she was pissed off, and the more he thought about it, he more than likely should have been a little afraid. But Christ, she was pretty all fired up like she was.

"You trying to buy your way into my bed?" His body went into overdrive thinking about all the things he wanted to do when he got her in the bed. "I don't have sex with strangers. And I certainly will never have sex with you. You're an asshole."

"Most of the time, yes I am. But I wouldn't discount the fact that you want me too." He moved quickly to kiss her and smiled. "But to be honest with you, I'm not ready to take you to my bed. I have patients to see as well as paperwork to fill out about the incident with your nephew. But in answer to your question, since I just met you and I have known him long enough to know that you're struggling, I don't think it's possible for me to have tried to buy my way into your bed. Do you think that it would be necessary?" He rocked hard into her again before kissing her on the nose.

Pulling away from her was the hardest thing he'd ever done. But he moved to the bed again and sat on the chair, careful to put the file in his hand on his lap. He was hurting, he was so hard, and his cat was making himself known about how his mate was standing right over there.

"Now, I wanted to ask you a few questions. And now that your aunt is awake, she can hear them as well." He handed Shane the first picture that the police had given him. He had to work extra hard to concentrate on what he was saying. All of him, every part of his body, wanted to grab the woman and take her to a dark and very quiet place to make her his. "This was taken from the video at the school yard. Can you tell me who this is?"

"Yes. His name is Walter Simpson. He's a senior at the high school where I go." Shane handed the picture to his aunt. "He's the one that beats me to snot a couple of times a week. He's also the one that cut me. He said that the next time, it would be my throat. I believe him, because there is a rumor around the school that he's killed before. I don't know if he has or not, but he sure is the scary type, don't you think?"

~~~

She had a hard time concentrating on what was being said around her. The man had touched her, licked her throat, and even kissed her. It wasn't a long kiss, just a

Nolan

meeting of mouths, but he had done more to her in that one— Christ, what was she doing even thinking about him? He was just a man. Nothing more, nothing less. But his cock had been more. Thick and hard, it had…. Rylee had to shake her body and mind to think of something else. It was the hardest thing she'd ever done. Then Shane said the boy had wanted to cut his throat.

"What did you say?" He told her again. "What for? Over some money? Did you tell him that you didn't have any? Or that he should get a job or something? I'm going to kick his ass."

Nolan laughed and she felt it all the way to her toes. He winked at her before he looked at Shane again, and she wanted to get up and pound him in the head. Then have him pound her with his cock. Rylee got up to pace and that didn't help worth shit. Now he was closer than he'd been when she'd been on the other side of the bed.

"The police want to talk to you and your aunt. I'm only here to verify for them that this is the man that hurt you. They're—"

Rylee focused on what he'd said. "What do you mean, man? He's a student. A kid like Shane is, right?" Nolan shook his head and started to speak. But she cut him off again. "You mean they just let anyone on the lot with a knife to cut on the students? What the fuck is wrong with—?"

"Could you please just shut up? And maybe just stop interrupting me so I can tell you what I know?" Rylee felt her mouth snap shut and was surprised that she didn't cut her tongue off when it did. Nolan had stood up when he spoke, and since she'd been pretty close to him again, she could see that they were a perfect fit in their bodies. Cock to pussy, chest to breast. And when he growled, it vibrated along her skin like he'd touched her with it. When he spoke, his voice was low and full of sex. She had never thought of that term before, but he was using it on her now. "You're not helping me one bit, so you know. But I have to finish this or we'll never get to your needs."

"My needs are just fine." He grinned at her, and she realized what that had sounded like. "What I mean is, you can talk to Shane, but you're to leave me alone. Forever. I don't have any use for you."

"Don't you?" Her face heated up. Nolan turned back to Shane, and she felt as if she'd been given some sort of reprieve or something. "But as I was saying. This is not a kid; a student, yes, but not a kid. He turned nineteen three months ago. He's been held back a few times."

"Why is he…? I'm surprised he didn't slit someone else's throat for that." She looked at Shane when he moaned. "I'm sorry, buddy. I really am. You know how my mouth gets ahead of my good sense sometimes."

"You said that before. I don't know what it means. But I know what you mean about this kid…man, I guess. Walter is one of the meanest people I ever met. Except for you when you get all worked up." He grinned at her. "Mom said that's why you liked the army so much. You could cuss with the best of them and make people do what you wanted all the time too. She called you bossy."

The pain of missing her sister was still there. How much they'd lost because neither of them had ever dreamed one of them wouldn't be around forever. Even in what she did with her life, it had always been assumed that she'd be the one that would die first, killed in the line of duty. But it had been her sweet, loving sister, Shelby, and not her, to suffer the way that she had. And she really did suffer needlessly, as far as Rylee was concerned.

As Nolan spoke to Shane, she tried her best not to think of her sister and the last months of her life. The pain she was in and the way she'd cried to her nightly about leaving her only child. Shane knew, Rylee was pretty sure, but he'd never said anything to her and she'd not mentioned it to him. Together they were a good team, she'd thought. At least until this came around. And right now she felt like a failure. Actually, that had come over her a great deal lately, the feeling of inadequacy. First the rent was always late, the car being taken, and now this. How the hell did people do it? Oh yeah, she thought, they didn't have forty-seven thousand dollars of hospital bills to pay, not to mention a funeral cost that was eating them alive every month. Nolan stood up, and so did she when he turned to her.

"The police are going to talk to you at noon. My brother Joey is going to come in and be here as well. He's an attorney." She wanted to ask him how many brothers he had but said nothing. "It'll be fine, Rylee. You'll see. You have support now, and we take care of each other."

"But I'm nothing to you." She watched his face and could see something there, but chose, for now, to ignore it. "You should just leave us to ourselves. We can...I'm not sure if you were serious or not about the bill here, but paying it will take us under. Well, it'll take us under faster than we're sinking now."

"I was serious. And it's been taken care of. Like I told Shane and now you, my bill and that of my brother, you don't have to worry about."

Nodding, she wanted to beg him to come back and hold her again, a feeling that she didn't have a lot of experience with, this need to be held. When he stopped at the door, she foolishly felt her heart pick up speed as he motioned for her to come to him with his finger. And like a bigger fool, she went to him.

The curtain at the door was closed, and before she could think or even decide if she wanted him to, he had her body pressed against the door and his mouth at hers. Christ, the man was making her crazy with need and desire.

The touch of his fingers over her breast made her look down. He'd lifted her blouse up and moved her bra out of the way for his touch. She moaned against his mouth when he thumbed her nipple. She tightened her hold on him as he moved down her body. As soon as his tongue laved her, she felt her eyes roll to the back of her head as the sensations nearly had her screaming out his name for more.

As he suckled at her, she curled her fingers into his hair, amazed again at how soft it was, and held him to her this time. He lifted Rylee by her ass, and she wrapped her legs around him like that was where they were supposed to be. He rocked into her now, hard like he was fucking her. His cock was hard, thick, and long. Rylee felt her mouth water to taste him, to feel him filling her.

"Christ, I need to taste you." She nodded, not sure if she had the ability to even speak when he whispered near her ear. "I want to bend you over something hard and take you. Eat your pussy until you're weak with your climaxes. Taste all of you, sample parts of you that are mine and mine alone."

His list of needs was just what she wanted as well. And when he nipped at her throat, she nearly screamed out his name, but a hard punch of a climax took her breath away. When he pulled his mouth from her flesh and stared into her eyes while he fucked her through their clothing, Rylee felt as if she was seeing her life, all of it, change in his stare.

"Come for me. Let me feel you come while I mark you." Nodding again, she held onto him, pulled him to her when she felt her climax racing up her body. "Come. I want to see your face when you release for me."

Her climax took her. Not only that, but she was sure it wasn't going to ever stop. His hand covered her mouth when she opened it to scream, and she pressed her hand over his when she thought her release might escape. When he leaned to her throat, his touch setting off another equally powerful release, she cried out against his hand over and over until she was dizzy from it. Just as he bit her, sank his teeth deep into her skin, Rylee came again, her body bowing back from the wall and tearing her asunder before things just slammed back together only to take her again.

Come. The word seemed to echo in her head as she came again. His voice seemed to be inside of her, over her, when he told her yet again to release. Rylee wanted to tell him she was finished, she couldn't take any more. But her body wasn't ready to quit just yet and came every time he told her to. Finally, weak beyond anything she'd ever been before, Rylee dropped her hands from his shoulders and knew if he hadn't been holding her up, she would have been a puddle on the floor.

He held her without saying anything. She expected...well, she had no idea what to expect from him, but knew that as a man, he'd say something mean. He'd given her more in these past few minutes than she'd had in all-nighters with a couple of men she had had sex with. When Nolan lifted his head from her neck, she could see a drop of blood on his lip and leaned forward to lick it off. She was shocked at it as soon as she tasted him on her tongue.

"You're mine." Her temper, never the best of things under normal circumstances, nearly took her breath away when he said that. But his hand over her mouth again prevented her from blasting him. "Your nephew is right behind this curtain, and there are any number of people in the hall. If you want to tear into me, then let's do it somewhere a little more private. Then maybe I can make you scream again before I bury my cock in —"

She hit him before she could think that she wasn't on her own two feet. And it wasn't one of those girly slaps where she might put an imprint on his face with her palm. It had been a punch that landed square on his nose and knocked him back, him taking her with him.

The curtain came down as he hit the floor. With her body still wrapped around his when she landed, Rylee could feel his cock between her legs. The need to ride him, free him so that she could feel him inside of her, made her angry with herself. Scrabbling to get off him, she stilled when he dug his hands into her hips and rose slightly from the floor. Rylee moaned before she could stop herself. Then her nephew laughed.

"Did you fall?" Did she? No, she'd been having the greatest sex she'd ever had with a stranger. But she looked up at Shane as Nolan held her still. "Are you guys hurt? Did someone open the door and knock you down?"

"No. We were having a discussion. And we're not quite finished yet. Are we, Rylee?" He purred her name, and she felt herself getting wet again. At his low growl, she got off him and made sure that she kneed him sharply as she did. *Not nice, love. And after I made you come so many times.*

"What did you do?" Nolan got up from the floor and she asked him again as he stood up, looking for all the world like a man that had been laid. "How did you do that?"

I bit you. Now we're connected. And you should talk to me like this. But this is something that we can talk about later. You're scaring Shane. She looked over at him and could see the worry on his face. Smiling at him, knowing that she didn't feel anything close to being happy, she sat on the bed next to him and looked at Nolan. His laughter through her head made her more pissed off. "I'll be back around two to see how things went. Like I said, Joey will be in to be on hand in the event you need him."

"Why?" Nolan asked her what she meant. "Why is he coming here to be on hand for anything? We have this under control. I have everything under control right now."

His hum, sort of saying, *do you really?* had her standing up. He only laughed again and left the room. Rylee had to count to ten four times before she felt she could say anything without screaming.

"You don't like him." Rylee looked at Shane when he spoke. "He's a nice guy, I think. And his brother is nice too. Do you suppose the other one will be too? Aunt Rylee, things will be all right, won't they?"

"I'm sure that they will be. But as for the brother, I have no idea." She must have been sharper than she'd meant to be and blamed that on Nolan as well. "I'm sorry. He's made you feel better, and that's all I care about right now."

"But you don't like him, do you?" She shook her head. "I do. And he was really nice to me in the office too. When I asked him about the cut, he didn't act like I was some kid that he had to lie to. He told me that I should have gotten help, and then told me that I was brave for finding it afterwards. Nolan wasn't like Mike. He listened to me and didn't treat me like some bug that he wanted to squash."

"Mike is an asshole. Do I do that to you?" He shook his head and lay back on the bed. "I'm sorry you got hurt, Shane. I had no idea that he was hurting you as badly as he was. I wish that you had told me."

"I really thought I could handle him. I mean, he's really big, but he's stupid too. And you said that fists never solved anything." Which was complete bullshit. She wanted to hit a good looking doctor again just to keep him away from her. "And, most of the kids in my class are afraid of him."

That didn't seem right either, and she wondered if the teachers were aware of it. When the police arrived at just before noon, she was ready to tell them to start, but Joey Bentley came in a few seconds after they arrived and told them he needed a moment with his client. Thinking it was her, she asked if he wanted her to go with him.

"Oh. I'm sorry. I'm here for Shane. My brothers think it might be best if he...." He grinned at her, and she took a step back from him. She had no idea why, but he really did sort of put her on edge too. "You're his mate? Nolan and you are...you're his mate. Well hot damn, that's the best news I've heard all day."

"I'm nothing to that arrogant bastard." Before she could tell him she was sorry for her outburst, Joey started laughing. "Are all of you men certifiable?"

"Pretty much. And welcome to the family." Then he started talking to the police about the man who had cut Shane. Rylee felt as if she were on a roller coaster that had more loops in it than a spring. And she had a feeling it wasn't going to get much better any time soon.

Nolan

Chapter 3

He kept forgetting what he was saying in mid-sentence. Nolan had to look down at the chart he was using with his patient and she suddenly laughed at him. Mrs. Jacobs was an old and dear friend of his mom's, and she was also a cat.

"Got you tied up in knots, I'm guessing. This girl of yours, you got yourself a good one?" He nodded and sat on the bed with her. She was dying, and soon too. Her age was undetermined, as she had made it perfectly clear she didn't want anyone to ever know that, so the chart had no year of birth but was a thick file on what she'd gone through as a panther.

"She's human, of course, and she's full of spit and fire. And I find myself pissing her off just to see her get that befuddled look in her eyes just before she tries to tear me a new ass." Mrs. Jacobs nodded and laid her head back on the pillows. "And she has a fourteen-year-old nephew that she's raising."

37

"No worries on that score, is there? I mean, you'll take him as your own." He told her he would. "Good. So much like your father. More than the rest of them boys. He was a good man, your dad. Always knew what to say and how to say it. Could be meaner than a snake when the mood took him, but kind as that wife of his when he needed that too. He did right by you boys and Gracie."

"Mom loved him with all her heart." She nodded and said that he would his mate as well. "I think I might have made her mad earlier. I marked her, as you know, but she's mad at me. And her nephew has had some run-ins with a bully."

"You'll get him straightened out. My boy, you remember Donnie? He had him some problems with one of them mean boys. When Donnie would try to ignore him, it only got him in more trouble. Teach this boy how to fight dirty. You should remember how to do that from your younger days." He tried to look shocked, but she snorted at him. "Seen you boys scraped up so bad when you were just cubs that it nearly tore into my heart. And that Howie would be egging you on like he was a ref in a big game. Never saw a man take on like he did when you...I don't think he's changed a bit either, has he?"

"No. He's still as ornery as ever. He usually started the fights by saying this or that about us. Working up things when they were not suiting him." Nolan laughed, and she touched her fingers to his cheek. "This girl, she's not had an easy time with it. They don't have any money from what Shane said, and they're struggling every week, he said, to have—"

"Shane Cole? And his aunt is Rylee McClure? They live down on Jefferson?" Nolan nodded, his cat ready to pounce should he need it. "Why, my goodness, you sure do know how to pick them. That girl has been working at my house now about…I guess it's been about six months. She's been helping me out around the house with some of the cleaning. They needed…boy, you know it when you say she's having some money problems. They got them a powerful bunch of them. And a neighbor that might need some dealing with. You should go on down there and take care of him soon."

"I'll do that today. I'll explain a few things to him. How bad is it, Mrs. Jacobs? I mean, I need to help her out. I have to help them." He made a mental note to go and talk to the neighbor today, before he went home. Looking back at Mrs. Jacobs, he could see that she looked so sad in the moment, and he took her hand into his. "Tell me."

"Shelby, her sister, had been married to this…I'm only calling him a man because he had the equipment to be one, not that I thought he was one. No man should…well, that's for later. Or for her to tell you. Anyway, about the time Shelby found out she was carrying that boy, he came along and tells her right out that he don't love her anymore. Never had, he said to her." Nolan asked her how she knew that. "Her mother was in my sewing circle. Nicest woman to come along. Anyway, she tells me about this man and his demands. Shelby was to never bother him for support or he'd take everything that she had, which at the time was a little bit. She was not to try and claim that boy of hers was his, either, or he'd make her life a living hell. And to say that he did would be a gross misunderstanding of the word hell. That man did things to them that made me so mad, I wanted to go and find that man and tear into him. But Cindy, Rylee's mom, just told me to wait, he'd get his."

"So that explains why there is no father's name on Shane's birth certificate. And did he get his? I certainly hope so." She shook her head. "Do you know him? Because I'm betting I can get him to get his."

"You do that. His name is David Cole. And when that boy was born, no more than a minute old, he came charging into the hospital and made her sign off on all forms of support from him. Even wanted her to sign off on the fact that she'd had an affair and that it was someone else's kid. But she wouldn't, and that's what they had to endure his whole life. David took things…well, I'm sure you'll find out sooner or later, but they didn't have a pot to piss in and no insurance. Not even sure they could have afforded it should they have had the inkling to have it. The lawyer fees just about took them under. Every time he had it in his head that something wasn't to his liking, he'd take her to court. Not about the boy, no sir, but about everything else. Took them everything to stay out of jail a couple of times."

"He tried to ruin her and that boy." It wasn't a question, but she nodded her answer anyway. "And for what reason? That he could? It was fun for him? What a bastard. I'll have Joey look into it, I think. And then she got sick. What did he do then?"

"There wasn't any money for doctors, so she…they didn't catch it until it was too late. When Cindy died a few months before Shelby got sick, her body just rotting away from the same thing, I guess it was hardest on Shelby because she'd cared for her momma while she'd been ill. Right up until she died too." Nolan nodded. "Rylee was sending home what she could. She didn't make a lot either, being in the service, and even reenlisted so that she could have the bonus money to give to her sister. But David, he took what he could of that too. Even had the house he'd said she could have taken out from under her by selling it off while they still lived in it. Never said a word until they were served the papers that it was done gone."

"Joey will love looking into this. He likes helping the underdog, even horses. He and Chris are already working with them on this bullying case." She nodded at him, and he watched her. As he started to get up to let her rest, she tightened her grip on his hand and started talking again.

"They don't have any money, Nolan. I don't mean they can't buy a movie ticket and popcorn kind of no money, but they more'n likely don't have the money for food or rent. And I know that what they're paying there is a good deal more than they should be. I'm thinking that bastard has something to do with that too." He asked her why she thought that. "I know what kind of man he is, and they're paying about a grand for that little bitty place that shouldn't be no more than two hundred if that. And since she can't come to my house and help me anymore…well, that wasn't much, but it helped keep the light on, she told me. Promise this old woman that you'll take care of them now. Not tomorrow, but now."

"I will. But convincing her, that might be an issue." She smiled a ghost of a smile as she drifted off. But he thought of something else and said her name softly. "Does she know what you are?"

"She does. More'n likely has an idea what you are too. She said that there are all kinds of animals in the world, and she knows on account of her job, but there were none that were nicer to her than I'd been. She's a good girl. And Shane is a fine boy. Your grandda, he'll just love him to death."

He left her then and started down the hall towards the next patient. He had three to visit today and wasn't looking forward to the next man. He was a cranky man that seemed to think that his impending death should be heralded as a national holiday that gave him the best. He was getting the best as far as Nolan was concerned, but the man demanded so much more.

But he didn't make it to his room because he heard his name called out over the PA to come to a room. He was running down the hall when he heard the voices coming from Shane's room. Christ, what had happened now?

Two officers were holding Rylee down. He really wasn't sure they were so much holding her as they were trying to hold her. She was going to break free from them soon, and Nolan could see hell was going to be paid when she was free. His mother and brother were there, of course, as well as Micah and Shane. He looked to be about as happy to see him as his cat was pissed off that someone was hurting his mate. Putting his fingers into his mouth, he whistled. The room seemed to freeze in motion.

"Now. I'm not sure what is going on here, but I would appreciate it if you unhanded her. Unless, of course, you want me to kill you both for manhandling my mate." The police jumped back from her like he'd hit them. Both the men were wolf and understood the meaning of mates. "Joey, want to tell me what the hell is —?"

"I'm standing right here." Nolan felt his cat snarl along his skin when she snapped at him. And when she came toward him, her temper blazing over her body, he wanted to pull her to him again and finish what they'd started earlier. "When you have a question that concerns me, ask me."

"All right. Rylee, my love, what the hell is going on here?" She snarled at him, and he nearly laughed, but he was pretty sure she would hurt him if he did. "I'm sorry.

You don't like small endearments? I will have to remember that in the future."

Micah laughed. It was loud and without boundaries, and he smiled at his older brother. That was when he noticed that his grandda was seemingly tucked in the corner and having just as much fun as Micah was.

"That man...that thing over there wanted to know why Shane had hurt the little shit that cut him up so badly that he needed thirty-seven stitches. And when I asked him where this...this other man was hurt, he said that it was none of my business. None of my business. Like it's all right for him to accuse my nephew of this heinous crime, but I can't know what it is he supposedly did to him?" She looked as if she might go after the officer again when Nolan stepped in front of him. "So help me, if you tell me to calm down I'm going to tear you up. I don't care what you are."

"I wasn't going to. I, like you, have a reason to live for a bit longer. I was actually saving the man behind me. You look like you could take him on without any trouble, but then we'd have to explain to his alpha why he was killed — and that's a lot of paperwork." She backed up but looked no less pissed. Nolan turned to Joey. "What does this other person say happened?"

"As I was getting ready to tell these two when the shit hit the fan, we have several witnesses that state that Mr. Simpson had been harassing Shane, as well as quite a few other boys, for months now. And my client didn't do anything more than defend himself." Joey tried to hide a grin but wasn't very successful at it. "Mr. Simpson's father is saying that young Shane here is the cause of all of this. And that, and I quote here, 'He should be stoned, then put to death.' I'm thinking that if we were in the dark ages, a stoning would kill him anyway. What do you think?"

"I am not the cause of anything. He tried to take my money. It wasn't much, but it was mine." Nolan looked at Shane and he flushed, his voice lower as he continued. "I was going to get Aunt Rylee a cake at the bakery on my way home. She's been so stressed out, and I wanted to get her one. But he took my money and then beat me up too. But I hit him this time. I was mad. But the knife, he never had one of those before, and he cut me with it."

"Of course you were mad." Grandda moved to the bed and patted Shane on the shoulder as he nodded, his voice full of compassion and love for the boy already. "I'd have beaten him to a pulp too had he tried that crap with me when treats were involved. What did you do to him, son? How is he thinking you hurt him as badly as he did you?"

"I hit him like Aunt Rylee did the man next door to us. It worked too." Shane grinned, then looked at his aunt and frowned. "I know you said that violence doesn't get you nothing but violence, but he was hurting me."

"What did she do?" Everyone turned to Micah when he asked, his voice harsh from trying not to laugh. "I heard this boy is about six-two and a good two fifty in weight. What did you do to make him run back to his daddy and tell on you?"

"I first popped him in the head with my forehead. That really hurt by the way, and I don't know how you did it to Mr. Packer without needing to lay down afterwards. Then I gave him the knee." Shane laughed. "Never seen a man go down so slow in my life. I had to...I might should have backed off a little when I did it, but I was so mad at him that I gave it all I had."

Joey turned to Nolan, his face bright with humor, and Nolan was having a hard time containing himself. When Joey turned to the cops, both of them standing there with their arms over their chests, Nolan thought he was going to tell them something funny. But in a heartbeat Joey's face changed to his game face, and Nolan felt sorry for the cops.

"As of right now my client is going to get a guard outside this room." When one of them started to speak, Joey simply raised his head. "You argue with me and the conversation I'm going to have with your chief is going to be one you'll never forget. And believe me when I tell you that you're going to regret your actions today. You are going to wish your name had never come up to come here. Get out of here now."

As the two of them shuffled out, Joey turned to Nolan. He could see the look in his eye now and it did not bode well for the bad guy. Nolan looked at Rylee when she spoke.

"Why? I mean, it's a done deal, right? This person is going to be suspended or whatever, and Shane will be all right." Joey was shaking his head, as he was. "No. This isn't right. They can't do this to him. To us. Tell me you're kidding."

"I wish that I was. And the school isn't going to be your biggest concern right now. Walter's father has said that if his son isn't treated well, then he'll take care of the little fuck that...sorry, but he's going to come after you as soon as he can." Joey glanced at Nolan before looking back at Rylee to tell her the rest. "The school is suspending only Shane for now, but I know someone on the board that has taken a great interest in this."

Grandda laughed before speaking. "Yeah, my Katie. You don't want to mess with her and family. She'll...she can be a mite on the mean side when she's all riled up, but once it's family? Well, I'd hate to be them." He looked at

Micah. "You gonna tell on them cops to that alpha? Have them brought in for disrespecting your family?"

"I've already spoken to him." Nolan wanted to ask how that had gone over, but Micah only shook his head. "Things are taken care of in that regard."

Rylee looked at him and Nolan wasn't sure what to tell her. When she sat down, he could see that she was feeling defeated. When she spoke, he knew she was.

"How is this even possible? He's the injured party in all of this." She looked up at him. "He's bigger, an adult, and he had a switchblade at school. How the hell is any of that even right, or them saying that Shane is the bad guy in this?"

"I don't know, love, but I intend to find out. Joey is going to help too. And as much as I'd like to tell you that I think you can handle Victor yourself, I think that you're going to need all of us to help you. And I know you're going to hate this, but I think it would be best if you moved in with me." She nearly fell leaping up from the chair, all signs of defeatist gone and the angry woman in her place.

"No fucking way." Shane, behind her, started laughing. Even Grandda did after a couple of seconds. Before Nolan could ask her to listen to him, the door behind them burst open and there stood Victor Simpson and his fucking bastard of a son.

~~~

Micah stood up and moved to the door. He knew this man…hell, they all did. He was one of the meanest men that ever walked the earth, and it looked as if the apple hadn't fallen far from the tree with the son. He came into the room like he owned it, and Micah was ready to show him that he did not when Rylee moved to stand by him.

"Your son hurt mine." Micah had thought that Shane was her nephew, but said nothing. "What the hell are you going to do about it?"

"Do? I don't think I understand there, little lady. You mean this scuff between the boys?" He laughed, but no one was fooled by his good old boy look. Not even Rylee, it appeared. "Well now, darling, we're going to settle this like adults. You pay off the little hospital stay here that your boy there caused, and I'll just pretend none of this happened. You know how boys will be boys. And this isn't nothing more than that. You just tell me how you want to pay for the damages and the hospital bill and we'll be on our way."

There was a long pause, and Micah thought that she wasn't going to say anything when she fanned her face with her hands and smiled. "Oh good. I thought for sure you were going to call me your sweetheart or some other bullshit name before you got to the fucking point." Victor looked at Micah as if he was confused. Micah said nothing. To be honest, he was enjoying this too much to say anything right now. "And as for your damages, as you called it, I'm not paying shit to you. As a matter of fact, I was going to have my attorney come to you about paying off Shane's. Good of you to save us some time."

"Now see here. I'm not paying a dime to you. That boy of yours should have been locked up instead of pampered in the bed like he didn't do anything wrong. Just look at my boy. He's been hurt and humiliated enough without you dragging a lawyer into this." Rylee snorted. "You might want to take it down a bit there, girl. I'm a big man in this town."

"You are at that. What do you weigh, three, three-fifty? I'm betting that you haven't pushed that bulk of yours away from the table before your platter was empty in years." She looked him up and down, and Micah had to put his hand over his mouth and bite hard on his hand to keep from getting himself hurt from laughing at either of them. Victor looked like someone had poleaxed him. Twice. "And have you looked at that son of yours? And so you know, males over eighteen aren't boys in this country, but full-grown adults, and he needs to be treated as one by the law for breaking it. Not pampered like you think my Shane is getting."

"Where is this paragon of goodness you call your nephew? Perhaps I want to hear his side of this story. Doesn't mean I'm going to change my mind, but I need to see right now what kind of kid you're raising. And don't think I don't know all about you either. I had you investigated, Captain Rylee McClure. You might have to take another job or two before I'm done with your ass." He laughed at her when she took a step forward, and Micah looked at Nolan. In that moment Micah was proud of his brother more than he'd ever been. He didn't move, and it looked to him like he was relaxed. Just on the outside he was sure, but for all appearances, Nolan was letting her handle this. For now, it seemed. "Well?"

Everyone turned to the bed. Micah kept an eye on the Simpson men, as did Nolan, but everyone else was staring at the bed. Victor turned to Rylee again and asked her if she was kidding.

"No. That's my nephew." In seconds she had turned from the bed and just blurred into action. She had flipped Simpson up and over her shoulder and to the floor in one fluid motion. Micah had never noticed the long knife she held at Victor's throat, and had no idea where it had come from. No one moved. Not even Nolan, who looked as if his cat was ready to attack. When Rylee spoke, her voice bespoke calmness and control of her temper. In no way did Micah think she was either. "You ever threaten me again or my status as his aunt, and I will hunt you down and show you what a real man is in the form of Captain Rylee McClure. I am not without my own means of making you pay, and I'm reasonably sure that my way is going to hurt you in ways you cannot even fathom."

When Walter moved to no doubt hurt Rylee, Nolan came up behind him and put him to the floor by bending Walter's arm up behind him and nearly to his shoulder. It was a good move, as Walter couldn't have moved without breaking his arm.

"Well now. This is going well, don't you think?" No one answered Joey as he pulled things from his briefcase. He, unlike the rest of the room, wasn't hiding his good humor. "Mr. Simpson...Victor...I wanted to let you know that as of this morning, I have filed charges against your son in the attempted murder of my client. Also, the school board has...well, after a long talk with my mom and grandmother, you are no longer a part of the board. It amazed all of us how much you had them under your control. Not anymore. Also, you should know that your bank accounts have been frozen in the event that you try to run or have your son try to run to avoid the other charges that are coming your way. It just tickled me to no end to have heard about all the reports of threats from you and your son that have come out in the last twenty-four hours."

"Nobody better be talking, or so help me they're gonna be sorry." Joey laughed, and Micah wondered just how many other complaints there were. "You let me up from here, girl, or so help me, I'm going to make it ten times harder on you than I first thought."

"Fuck you." Shane laughed on the bed and his aunt turned to him. "I hear you repeating any of these curse words and I'll wash your mouth out with lye soap. And trust me when I tell you, that is not going to make you any better."

"Yes, ma'am." Shane looked at Grandda when he leaned in to speak to him. In seconds they were moving to the bathroom, and Grandda was standing outside the door. It was time to move, and Grandda was making sure that Shane was ready when they did.

"Now Mr. Simpson. I'm going to lift my body off yours and you are going to let me. If you don't, you're going to die. That's not a threat but a full-out promise. I can cut you in ways that will make you beg for death, or end you right fucking now. Do you understand what I'm saying?" He called her a lot of names, and it wasn't until a small drop of blood trickled down his throat that Micah realized that she could and would hurt Victor without a backward thought. "Do you understand me?"

"You're going to pay for this. And money, not that you have shit, is not going to be what I'm going to take from you." The knife went deeper and the blood started to flow quicker. "Yes, I understand you're going to get up. Just get off me, cunt."

"That's Rylee. Or McClure. Mostly that's what my men called me. Don't call me cunt again, Victor, or I will hurt you."

She moved slowly and he didn't touch her. When she was by Nolan, Micah moved quickly, putting his hand around Victor's throat where the knife had been. The man wasn't talking now, not that he could have, but Micah could see fear in his face, not the contempt that he had shown for Rylee. No matter how misplaced it had been.

"You touch her or anyone in my family again, and I will ruin you." Victor had started to turn blue before Micah let up on his windpipe. "I'm not going to ask you if you understand me. I'm hoping that you do and just don't give a shit enough to come after me and mine."

Walter was released too, but he didn't move to help his father up. It was comical the way the man had to maneuver to just get to his knees. Then it took him another few minutes to stand up, his breath coming in hard short bursts. When he turned to Rylee, she grinned at him like she knew just what he was going to say.

"You're dead. Do you understand that, you fucking cunt? Dead." As he turned she said his name. Micah wasn't sure what she was going to say to him, but when she reached down and grabbed him by the balls and lifted him up with her hand, gripping them tightly, he screamed like a little girl.

"You want to rethink that line of thought, you worthless piece of fuck. I've been trained to kill a man as quietly or as loudly as I can. And the screaming is from my victim, not from me." When she let him go and he moved back, Rylee spoke again. "Either of you come near my nephew again and you'll never see me kill you."

As soon as the Simpson men were out of the room, Rylee dropped to her knees. She didn't move, even when Nolan moved to stand near her, other than to lean her head on his leg. Nolan looked at Micah.

"Can we come stay with you until I can work out somewhere to live, as well as some security?" Micah nodded. "Thank you. We should leave now. I don't think...he's going to come back as soon as he can think beyond how painful his balls are right now." He looked down at Rylee, who had not said a word since the Simpson's had left. "Remind me never to piss you off."

Her laughter made everyone in the room relax a bit. Shane came out of the bathroom dressed in his bloodied clothing and went straight to his aunt. These two, Micah realized, were going to need a great deal before this was finished. And he had an idea that his mom was going to love every minute of this story when he told her and Reggie.

Chapter 4

Reggie showed the two of them up to their rooms. She wasn't really sure where Nolan was going to be staying while they were here, but she assumed with Rylee. She already smelled like him, so she had been confused when he'd dropped them off earlier telling them he'd be back. When Rylee turned to her, she could see that the woman was as confused as she was.

"What's going on?" Reggie asked her what she meant. "I mean, don't get me wrong, this is an amazing house, but I don't know what the hell...heck I'm doing here. Or for that matter, why you're treating me like a long lost friend that you've not seen in ages."

"You are my friend. I know you're aware of what we are—shifters—but do you understand that you're Nolan's mate?" The nod and the shaking of her head didn't surprise Reggie one bit. "Yeah, I know just how you feel on that part. I sort of kinda knew what a shifter was, but not that they were too. And when I found out that Micah was not

53

just my mate but…well, the Bentley men can be a bit to take sometimes. They're very bossy."

"So am I. But that doesn't answer my question." Rylee sat on the bed, then hopped back up when Gracie entered the room. They'd been introduced before at her house, and now Gracie was handing her a stack of clothing. "What's this?"

"Nolan just called to ask me to see if there was anything I could lend you to wear. But Chris was here and already had a few things for you. And so you know, we've found something for young Shane to wear as well. Poor thing had nothing but a bloodied shirt to put on. Oh, and Burke has looked at him and he's going to take a pain pill and lay down. Shane, not my Burke." Gracie sat on the chair. "I think I can answer your questions too. And Chris will be up. She's a witch, darling, so please bear that in mind when she talks to you. Not that she'll change you into anything…I'm not even sure if she can, but knowing her, she—"

Reggie cleared her throat, and Gracie just grinned at her. Chris entered the room then with Katie, her grandmother-in-law. Reggie wondered how they looked to Rylee. A bunch of women here to gang up on her, or a friendly family gathering of the women folk? Either way, they could be and were more than likely very overwhelming.

"We're panthers." Chris looked at her when Rylee sat down. "I'm sorry, should I have been gentler with that?"

"No dear, you did fine." Gracie moved to sit next to Rylee. "I'm to understand that you're aware of shifters. And that you know Mrs. Jacobs. Nice woman. She's a patient of Nolan's…did you know that?"

"No. She's been sick for...what am I doing here?" Gracie glanced at Reggie before answering Rylee. "I understand that that bast...that man is going to try and exact some revenge, but I can take care of myself. It's money that I have issues taking care of."

"Well, you are Nolan's mate, first of all. Not that that isn't a great thing, but there are things going on that you need to be made aware of. Do you know much about Victor Simpson?" Reggie thought about what Micah had told her about the meeting with the Simpson men and laughed a little. "His son isn't much better, I'm told."

"I don't know either of them other than what I figured out on my own today. They're not nice men." Chris laughed, and Rylee turned to her. "You're really a witch?"

"Yes. Very much so. And you should know that I can read your mind too." Rylee took that better than she might have under the circumstances. "Also, you should know that the moment you entered into this relationship with Nolan, you became what he is. Not the panther part of him, but the rest."

"The rest?" No one answered Rylee, but she got up to pace. "My nephew, he's going to have to be made safe above anything that prick might...that man might do to me."

Reggie thought it was funny that Rylee immediately curbed her language. When the monitor in her pocket made a noise, she excused herself and stood up. Gracie said she'd go too, and they left to get her daughters. Reggie both hated and loved nap time. She missed them while they were down, but needed them to take a nap so she could rest too. They were such a joy to have, but exhausting. When she and Katie came back, each of them with one of the girls in their arms, it looked as if the other women had gotten no further than they had before she'd left them.

As Rylee paced the room, Alexis and Anne were played with. Reggie was sure that Rylee would have a lot of questions, but for now, she seemed to be content to walk off her frustrations. When she stopped and turned to her, she felt her cat stir at her skin.

"You're not going to shift, are you?" The fact that she was aware that she might have shifted startled Reggie. She'd been told that only another paranormal could tell that, and maybe a few humans. When she told her that she wasn't, but her cat was a little nervous, Rylee nodded before continuing. "I'm guessing that one or all of you know what Shane and I have been going through?"

"Yes. Joey told Micah what he'd been able to find on you when he took the case, and he told us so that we'd be better equipped to help out. Nolan also talked to Mrs. Jacobs at the hospital. About your ex-brother-in-law. David Cole is on our list, too." Rylee snorted at her. "You don't believe me?"

"Oh, I believe that you know about some of the stuff we've been going through, and maybe Chris knows a lot more, but what you don't know is that I'm a total screw up at this parenting thing." Gracie asked her who told her that. "Shane. Not so much in words, but have you seen what that bas...that guy did to him? Beat him up, and I went on like nothing was going on."

"You cannot fix what you're unaware of." Again, Rylee snorted, at Katie this time. "My husband does that. I would think that you taught him, but he's been doing it a good deal more and more lately. I don't care for it any more from you than I do him. If you have a comment or something profound to say, then please do so. But we have work to do and we need your help to get it done."

"I've spent the last eleven years of my life in the service, ma'am. I have said more things, done more than that, than most people do in a lifetime. And right now I'm trying to be a mother to a motherless boy and doing a really shitty job of it." Rylee stretched her neck and it popped twice before she looked at Katie. "Had I a single clue what the hell I was doing, none of this would have happened and we'd be living out our lives on the edge of disaster without the Bentleys being aware of it."

"Oh no, that's not true. Sooner or later you and Nolan would have met." Chris smiled at Rylee when she asked her how. "The fates. They have a hand in most of our lives, and more in that of a shifter. You were meant to be his mate, and no matter how much you would have tried to avoid it, you still would have been mates."

"And if I hadn't been there, you're saying that something else would have brought us together?" Chris nodded. "Well, I call it bullshit. I think everyone has choices, and mine is to be without a mate."

"Yeah, well, it's a little too late for that, my dear." Katie stood up and laid the baby on the bed before looking directly at Rylee. "You are doing a wonderful job, my dear. And Shane knows that. He got hurt. It happens. But he's not dead. Dead is very hard to fix."

No one said anything, but Reggie knew they were all dealing with their own form of grief. All of them at some point had lost someone they loved. And losing Micah, her son, had been hard on Katie and his mate, Gracie.

The pacing began again, and Reggie wondered what sort of things were going on in Rylee's head. When Chris touched her mind, she smiled at the other woman, knowing that she had heard her mind asking.

She's afraid for Shane. And for Nolan. She has it in her head that he's going to hear something that he's not going to like and throw them to the wolves, so to speak. Reggie asked her if she loved Nolan yet. *No. They're not at that part of their bonding, as you know, and she's not going to be that easy to convince, I think. Army life has taught her to mistrust a great deal more than you and I take as the truth. Shane, she feels, might be better off without her.*

That's ridiculous. Chris told her it was no more so than her being able to read others' minds. *But you can do that. It's not the same at all.*

But it isn't to her. Reggie could see her point in that. But there was no way that that kid down the hall was any better off without her. *We have to do something.*

We are. We're here for her. They both turned to Rylee when she stopped moving. Reggie was almost afraid to ask Chris what she was thinking now. But Rylee spoke first.

"Nolan is at my old place. He just asked me what I needed from there. Is that normal?" Gracie told her that he'd want her to have things that were hers to make her feel better. "Yeah, I got that part, but he's speaking to me from my apartment. Not here in the room with me, but from...I think I need a drink."

Miss May came in a few seconds later with more than just the tea trolley loaded with an assortment of cookies, scones, and tea. She also had a large bottle of Kentucky's finest. Reggie thought for sure that Rylee was going to just drink from the bottle, but she poured it into the glass that Miss May handed her from her pocket.

When she poured enough in the glass to fill it up, Reggie laughed. It was going to be fun watching this woman tame Nolan. Because as much as she loved the mild mannered Nolan, this woman was going to shake him to his very core.

~~~

Joey looked around the large spacious room he'd been set in. There were things in this house that he was sure might have been here longer than his family had been around. He looked at the painting over the mantel and had to smile. The man there was a notorious rake and had been wonderfully flamboyant at it. He knew a great deal about the Cole family now.

"He's my great so-many-times-I-lost-count grandfather. Terrible husband, but the women loved him. Almost as much as men hated him for it." Joey turned to look at the grand dame Mrs. Cole. "I don't usually entertain men I don't know, but I talk to your grandmother all the time and thought I should meet with you. What can I possibly do for a man such as yourself, Joseph?"

Joey felt his face heat up. He wasn't one to be embarrassed easily, but she'd done it with a few words and a sexy wink. He knew that she was in her late eighties, but he would bet anything few knew that fact.

"I'm here on behalf of your...I would guess your great-grandson, Shane Michael Cole." She asked him to sit when she did. The butler came in with a silver tea service with a C on the front of it. When he'd finished serving them, he left them alone.

"I don't have any grandsons. My...whatever David is to me in a long line of disappointments, he only has daughters. And they're not worth the sweat it took him to plant them in that equally disappointing wife of his." Joey sipped his tea and asked her about Shelby Cole. "Shelby? I've not...that girl was also a sad disappointment. That boy, it's not his, he said. Had her sign off on something or another to say so."

"Do you believe him?" It was a chancy question and one that could very well get him thrown out even before he began this. "I believe that not only is Shane his son, but that David has made his life and that of his mother up to and after her death very difficult. There are things you might not be aware of that I have information on."

"And if he is? What does he want? In my will, I suppose? Does this child have plans to ruin David?" Joey said nothing but reached into his briefcase and handed her paperwork. "What's this?"

"DNA reports on Shane. Also, you'll find pictures of him. I see the resemblance and I think you will as well. There is also a transcript of the conversation that David had with his wife, Shelby, while she was still in recovery after Shane was born. The hospital has the original and the recording if you don't believe me." Joey handed her another thick file as well. "He sold the house that they were to have after the divorce. And should she sign the paperwork stating that she'd had several affairs while married to David, he promised her a monthly settlement. There was never any money given to her or her son. Of course, she hadn't had any affairs either. She was as loyal to David as he was at having the affairs. Copies of all of those, including the ones she did sign, are in that as well. When she wouldn't play ball his way, he took more from them. David is — and I think I have a good case for this — directly responsible for her not getting the treatment that she needed, and the added stress shortened her life considerably."

Mrs. Cole said nothing but looked through the file. He knew when she got to the pictures of the boy, and knew that she could see how they looked alike as well. Meanness had made him include a copy of not just Shane's birth certificate, but also a copy of the death certificate of his mother, as well as copies of the still unpaid bills that had mounted up over her illness, including the cost to bury the young woman. He had been surprised by the amount of money that Rylee had been settled with, and wanted to help her out even more.

Mrs. Cole laid them on her lap and said nothing for several minutes. He let her think. Joey knew it was a great deal to hand someone. When she finally looked at him, Joey knew that he'd messed up and that all of this was in vain.

"You never answered me, Joseph. What does this boy…and his aunt want from me? I'm assuming they know that there is money to be had if this is true." He shook his head. "They don't want my money? Or David's? I understand his current wife has plenty enough to allow him to have numerous affairs and vacations to wherever he wants. Perhaps if you enlighten me on what it is they do want, we can move on from there."

"They don't know I'm here." She nodded and picked up the little bell on the tray. When the butler appeared just after the bell was set down, Joey stood up. "I'm sorry to have wasted your time."

"Do sit down, Joseph. I dislike having a man…any man…assuming that he knows my mind. I'm very old and very good at getting things done as well. You'll see that in a moment." She turned to the butler. "Call Jenkins and tell him to get his ass here now. And tell him to bring what he needs to clear up a paternity suit."

The butler looked shocked for all of a second before telling her he would make the call. Joey could only imagine what was going through his head at that moment, and leaned back in his chair and looked at the very wealthy and slick woman.

"David is not going to be happy with you." She snorted. "I'm sitting here wondering if you might have known about this all along. I hope not. But I need to know."

"You don't need to know jack shit." He laughed at her and she smiled. "No. I didn't know. Had I known any of this I might have taken some sort of action. I guess...David has been somewhat of a problem child of late. I know that his wife—I have no idea what her name is—is looking for ways to get out of this marriage. There was a pre-nup that she wanted him to sign, but I'm reasonably sure that like with Shelby, he made himself come out on top of that as well." She sipped her tea and leaned back in her seat. "Tell me, young man. This boy, is he...is he doing all right now? I mean, I know he has lost his mother, but other than his grief, is he well?"

"Not really." She nodded and looked sad. "He and his aunt are currently staying with my brother and his wife. One of my other brothers, Nolan, asked me to look into this for the sole reason of making David acknowledge his son. As for your money, you know my family well enough to know that we've no use for yours or David's. It's the...I guess you could call it the principle of the matter now."

"Yes, I can see that. And as for the money, I should have thought before I spoke out of turn. But when you become as jaded as I have been of late, you think things before asking questions. As for all of this, I'll do what I can without...these bills, are there more? Is there something I can do to help them...? I need to help them. Can you tell me how they are faring?" Joey nodded and pulled out yet another file. "I'm impressed with you. I should like for you to come and work for me."

"I have plenty to do now, but I thank you. If you do need me, however, my wife and I can help you. But as for full time, I have a ranch that we're working and a baby on the way." She smiled at him and told him congratulations. "Thank you. Chris and I are extremely happy."

She was still looking over the file that he'd given her last as well as looking over the other files when the doctor arrived. They had moved to the dining room. The table there was large enough to accommodate the files she'd spread out, as well as the pictures she'd had Kason, her butler, bring to her of David.

Dr. Jenkins didn't ask her what it was about, just took a swab of her mouth and a few hairs, and even a sample of her blood. When she told him that she wanted it fast, he said that he could have it in forty-eight hours. Taking the copies of Shane's bloodwork with him, he was gone ten minutes after he arrived.

"I would very much like to meet them." He said he wasn't sure that was a good idea until they knew the results. "You know as well as I do that Shane is David's. And I'm going to make sure...well, let me just say to you that David will know that I do not like to be lied to. I would...can your family handle a few repercussions? He'll be pissy and want revenge. Also, it wouldn't surprise me if he tried for custody now that it'll come out. I'd...I'd like to suggest that your brother marry the aunt and adopt the boy as soon as possible. There'll be no change on my end should he do this. But as far as the courts go, it will go better for them all."

Joey told her he'd talk to them. "As far as you meeting them...I'll have to talk to them. As I said, Nolan asked me to look into this and I said that I would." She asked him again why. "Because of David's treatment of the mother,

Shane has lost everything. I do realize that he's never had much so it wasn't much of a hardship on him concerning the material things. But his mother did suffer at David's hands. They were left without any kind of support, nor did they even have a home until Rylee, Shelby's sister, mustered out of the service to come home and work while caring for them. Sometimes as many as three jobs at a time just to make the rent. And there were plenty of times when there simply wasn't any food."

"He wants revenge." Joey nodded. "Good. I like a man that will go the extra mile to make things right for his family. And you coming here…that makes me think you like this Rylee as well."

"Yes, ma'am. She's going to…she and Nolan have some things to work out, but I think in the end, it will." She asked if Rylee was human. "Yes she is, for now. How did you know?"

"I told you, I know your grandmother. And there is a pistol if I ever met one." Joey asked if she meant Katie Bentley. "Oh my, the stories I could tell you about her in her younger days. And Howie? That man…well, that is for another time. But you should ask them about the cruise that our families took together. That will give you a whole new view into your grandparents."

Joey left with the promise of getting in touch with her in a few days. And she told him that if she got the results back sooner, which she said she would, she'd let him know. Joey had a feeling things were going to be just peachy around the Cole household in a few days.

I just left Mrs. Cole's home. And she is a believer. It took her about five minutes to have her doctor come in and get a sample from her. Nolan thanked him again, but Joey could hear the frustration in his voice. *What's going on? Something happened?*

Yes. I have to...I'm going to take Rylee over to the shelter today. Mom mentioned the charity thing and she said that I should take her. Sounded reasonable, but not enough to frustrate him on it. *I didn't think to ask her to this thing, and she's sort of put out that she needs to use my money to buy a dress.*

Put out or pissed? He told him both. *Good. You should have told her about it. Not to say that you haven't had a lot on your mind, but you need to be more open with her. Have you...have you bonded yet?"*

It was a personal question, he knew that, but he also knew that things were moving much faster than Nolan was moving right now. Joey understood that he wanted to help her understand things, but if David Cole came for them, they had to all be ready.

Are you going to try and tell me how to do this too? Joey wasn't sure what to say to Nolan, so he didn't say anything. His temper of late was touchy, and it seemed to take very little to set him off. *I'm sorry. I have...this isn't going well here. I have to get a house, and I don't have the funds right now. And please don't tell me you can give them to me. I'd like to do this on my own.*

Nolan, what's wrong?" He'd asked him that before, and had, in the past, gotten either a nasty answer or none at all. He was expecting them both right now. *I want to help you.*

I've been...stupid. Joey wasn't sure he could have disagreed with him so kept his mouth shut. *I don't know what to do. I'm not even sure I know what's wrong with me. Maybe...maybe I'm just...I don't know. Joey, I'm afraid.*

Of what? He wanted to reach out to his brother and look into his head. He could now, thanks to the magic that he'd gotten from Chris. But he was afraid to. He wasn't sure what he'd find when he looked. *What are you afraid of, Nolan? Tell me.*

I'm such a disappointment. Before he could speak, shock making him speechless, Nolan said he had to go. *I'm going to the shelter today so that I can show Rylee what you guys have done. Later.*

The connection wasn't just closed, but seemed to be slammed shut. He tried twice to reach Nolan but until he was sure, he wouldn't hurt him by forcing his way in. He was going to talk to Chris first.

He reached for his grandda, knowing that if anyone could help him it would he him. Grandda, of course, had plenty to say, but very little of it was going to be helpful.

You leave him to me. I'll talk to your grandmother too. She can do all kinds of things that we menfolk can only think about. She'll bring that boy…what did he tell you that makes him think…? Good heavens, he's a doctor. How would…? It's this shelter thing. I knew it. I'll talk to him.

Joey was a little nervous now. Pushing the gas pedal a little harder, he wondered if he'd made a mistake talking to Grandda. Wondering what else could possibly go wrong, he made his way to Micah's house to talk to him.

Chapter 5

Rylee looked around the shelter. It was nicer than their last home and a good deal better equipped. There was a small store that people could come to and use credits to purchase things like soap and toothpaste. The credits were earned by doing chores around the building, from sweeping to washing down the bathrooms.

"I thought it would give them some worth. And there is a list where they can sign up to take turns running the store, too. I even offered to have potential job seekers use it as a sort of part-time job to put on resumes." He frowned and she waited for the put down, as she'd begun to call them. "My mom suggested that we put in the extras like laundry items. I was just going to give them to them, but she said that it gave them something that would be theirs, paying for items that they needed."

"This thing? Is it a family project then?" He didn't answer her, and she stopped him from moving again. "Nolan? What is going on here? Your mom tells me you have this great plan and what it's doing for the community. You tell me that it's your family's, and that other than the start up, you have no part of it. I'm still trying to figure that one out since everyone but you says it's yours. And there is the way you keep telling me that it's not what you wanted. What is it you wanted? To have your name engraved on each wall and floor?"

"I started it some time back. And then when my family found out about it, they sort of barged in." She knew it was more than that and asked him again. "I had gotten myself down to being broke. Not just where I couldn't pay for all the things here, but I wasn't going to be able to pay my rent on my apartment. So they came in and took over."

"Took over, or you gave up?" He didn't say anything, but she knew that she'd touched a nerve by the look on his face. "What have you done to help them, when this was your project and they've helped you out?"

"Nothing." It sounded defensive, and she felt her own temper rise up to meet his. "You should know that I'm a big disappointment to them. Getting myself in a hole that I can't get myself out of."

Rylee hit him. Not hard, but enough to get his attention. She could tell that his cat was close…it was almost as if she could touch him, but he needed his head put back in place, and she was going to do it. Taking his arm, she dragged him over to two men that were standing there acting like they had nothing to do but hold up the broom that one of them was holding.

"This man, do you know him?" The bigger of the two of them shook his head. "He's the one that started this thing. His family is helping him out."

"Yeah, that's Nolan Bentley. Did you know that they're going to have food here? And a place I can shower every day instead of when I can get me into a station with a sink." He nodded to Nolan. "I'm even working today."

"Good for you." She moved to the next group of men and woman. "This is Nolan Bentley. He is the one that purchased this building and started this project before his family came in and took over."

"Family is good. You don't get but one chance to have a good one. Them helping you, they's made it so we can have a nice place. Thank you for getting us a warm dry place to sleep and live again." The man standing there shook his hand.

The woman spoke next. "You got us the beds too, I heard." Nolan nodded and told her how they'd been stored in a warehouse that he'd purchased. "A bed. Do you know how long it's been since I slept in one? More'n I like to think about. Thank you."

As they moved deeper into the building, she could see the doctor's office as well as a pharmacy. She knew that he'd done that; his mother couldn't say enough about the things that had been in place before they'd come to help him. She stopped by the day care and looked inside at the two people in there setting it up, as well as a handicapped young man playing with the paints.

"He came in three days ago. That's what came up when Shane was in my office. There were some problems about him wanting to paint all day and there is this schedule to follow. I had to intervene on his part. The boy's mother and father had kicked him out when it was too hard for them to care for him." She asked him who had let him come here now. "I did, like I said. The offices that we passed, there are going to be doctors in all the time. A dentist friend of mine is also going to make visits here. We're even going to have someone come in for the kids that need help."

"An after school program. Your mom told me about it." He nodded and leaned against the wall to look at her. "You started this project, I'm aware of that. But do you think that any of them, your family, would have done this without your help?"

"I didn't ask for their help." She huffed at him. "Did Micah put you up to this? Tell you to bring me down here and try and make me see reason?"

"Fuck you. Do I strike you as a person that can be told what to do?" He laughed and told her no. "Tell me something, Nolan. What would your father say to you if he could see the way you're acting right now?"

"He'd be disappointed in me. Tell me that I'm a fool for sitting around on my ass and whining about what I'm not doing." He turned to look around the massive room. "I've been thinking about what he'd say for a week now. But I'm in over my head in coming back to this. I can't...they don't need me."

"Really? And why the hell do you think that?" He didn't answer her, and she jerked his head around to look at her. "Why do you think that your family, who would die for you, doesn't need you?"

"Because I'm whiny and a pain in the ass." She told him that she got that. "Are you always such a pain in the ass?"

"Pretty much." He pulled her to his body, and she went willingly. To have this man touch her gave her feelings she'd never had before. "You should know that I'm just as much a disappointment to Shane as you think you are to your family. He might have been better off in the system as much as I'm not doing for him."

The swat to her ass brought her closer to his body. His cock stretched now, and she could feel it thicken as he held her to him. When he cupped her ass and brought her as close as she could be without being naked and him inside of her, she moaned.

"I want you. Right now, I'd like nothing better than to find us a room with a lock on it and ravish you." His mouth took hers. It wasn't a kiss so much as a claiming. He was making sure she knew that she was his. "My cat would like to taste you as well. Drink from your wet pussy until he can mark you as his."

"Nolan, there is nowhere for us to go, and I hate to have you satisfy me and not yourself again." He growled, and her body responded to the sound. "Help me, please. I've only thought of you inside of me for days. Will you fill me, Nolan? Will your cock fit inside of me?"

This time he jerked her along the long stretch of the middle of the building. When he opened a door, she could see that it was some kind of storage room and wasn't surprised when he nearly tossed her inside before following her and closing the door. The lock sounding had her breathing double and her heart rate pounding.

"Take off your clothes. I want to see you before I eat you." She wanted to argue with him. The room was small, the only hard surface was the smallish table that sat in the middle of the room. "If you don't take off your clothing my cat is going to make short work of them, and you're going to be naked with nothing to put on when we're done."

Taking off her blouse, she dropped it on the floor. The bra was next. Slipping her pants down with her panties, she was naked in less than ten seconds. And when he told her to sit on the table, she did so without question.

"I'm going to fuck you after I have my fill. And when I do I'm going to bite you, mark you. Will you do the same to me?" He took off his shirt and his belt. She watched him, her pussy heating up so hot that she wanted to touch herself to see if it was as hot as she thought it was. Nodding to him, she watched as he pulled open his pants, his cock outlined in his briefs as he kicked them across the room. "Don't run from him. If you do, there is going to be a lot of people seeing you like you are now."

The cat simply consumed him. She felt the hairs on her arms dance. The magic or whatever it had been that had changed him made her think she was in trouble. As the large cat moved toward her, she opened her legs and let him sniff her. As soon as he licked her from gate to clit, she knew she was going to really enjoy herself. Lying back on the table, she felt his breath on her thighs and nearly came when he buried his nose into her.

Cupping her breasts, she tugged at her nipples as the cat feasted on her. Every time his tongue would touch her clit, she could feel the roughness of it and rolled her hips up to meet each of his strokes. Each time she came, which were too many to count, he would lap at her, taking the cream away almost as quickly as she felt it gush from her body. And when his tongue entered her, fucking her with sharp, hard strokes, she came screaming out Nolan's name and felt the room simply tilt and rock around her. Then Nolan was there.

~~~

Her body was tone, her breasts red from her hands. Nolan leaned in, his cock in his hand, and suckled at her nipple, making the hard little morsel tender before he bit down on it. Her hand at the back his of his head brought him closer, and he opened his mouth wider and took as much of her flesh into his mouth as he could before biting her again. Nolan wanted to eat her too, but the thought of being deep in her body was making him lightheaded with need.

Her hips moved up to his groin. The heat there, even before he slid his cock over her, was enough to make him wonder how hot she was going to be inside. As he soaked his cock with her juices, he slid just his crown into her and nearly came when she rolled her hips again and her sheath seemed to suck him in. Nolan rolled his own hips and filled her to the root of his being. Her nails digging into his arms made him pause and look down at her.

"Christ, you're wonderfully full." He grinned and leaned in to kiss her. It was difficult not to move, to rock into her as he tasted her dark mouth. Lifting his head just a little, he rocked forward and watched her face. It was beautiful, but now, with her so close to the edge of coming, she was too gorgeous for words.

"My cat loved the way you gave him what he wanted." He moved again, taking her closer still as her ankles locked behind him. "Next time, we're going to go to the woods behind my brother's house and I'm going to run you down before I let him taste you."

"Fuck me, Nolan, please?" He moved again, slower than before, and she cried out in frustration. "If you don't fuck me so I can come, I'm going to do it myself." He lifted his body from hers, his cock still inside of her, his hands holding her hips. Nolan watched her fingers as they slid down her skin. He was mesmerized by the dance that she showed him, and he began fucking her harder now. But as soon as her fingers entered her pussy with his cock, he growled low. She'd been tight before, but now it was as if she was strangling his cock.

Holding her legs open wider, he pounded her. Her fingers were sliding over her clit and touching his cock every time he moved in and out of her. The sensation was amazing, and when she bowed up and screamed, his own climax nearly took his breath away. As it was, he'd had to hold onto her so as not to be bucked off. Leaning to her throat, he begged her to come again and bit her when she screamed out his name. Her mouth, near his shoulder, sank into his skin even as his own mouth filled with blood as he marked his mate. They were one, and would be for the rest of their long lives together.

Nolan fucked her slowly. He was still hard, his cock empty, but the thought of pulling from her body and the idea that he would have to soon anyway made him want her all the more. As she held him, her body rising up to greet his made him smile down at her.

"You are pretty good at this. How many people do you suppose heard us?" He told her he didn't care. "Yeah, me either really. I'm guessing that this biting thing, it's going to be an ongoing sort of happening with us too?"

"Yes. Does it bother you?" She only smiled at him as he fucked her harder. "I'd very much like to bite you again while you come. To hear you saying my name is the biggest turn on I've ever experienced."

"You should know that when your cat was eating me, I fully expected him to bite me too. Is he going to be a part of our sex too? I don't...I won't have to have him fuck me, will I?" He sat up now and lifted her so that she was wrapped around him. Turning, he sat on the table this time and lay back when he was sure that she was safe on top of him. "Oh Christ, Nolan. You're so fucking thick."

"Ride me. And in answer to your question, yes, he'll want a part of you too, but not to fuck you. If you let me convert you, he'll fuck your.... Holy shit! Yes, again." She rolled her hips over him, and when she leaned down and took his nipple into her mouth, he felt his vison blur for a few seconds while she suckled him as he had her. "No, he won't fuck you, but if you keep that up, your ride is going to be short."

She moved back and forth over him. Her eyes were closed and her hands were at her breasts again. He wanted to taste them as she rode him, but he wanted to see her face too. Rylee was enjoying herself, and he didn't want to take away from her enjoyment.

"Someday I'd very much like for you to let me suck your cock." He rolled his hips up, unable to stop himself. "Then when you're ready to come, I want you to jerk off so that you come all over my face. I've never done that before, but with you, I think it would be fantastic."

"Now." She looked down at him, her hands stilled at her nipples. "I'd very much like to come all over you like that now. Having you suck my cock while I fuck your mouth is…Christ, woman, you're going to kill me."

She moved off him gently. His cock ached from being so full again and not releasing, but when he sat up, she leaned over him and took him deep into her throat even before he could get to his feet. And when she swallowed, he knew he wasn't going to go much longer.

Her mouth was as hot as her pussy had been, and tight around his cock. Every time he went past the tight muscles at the back of her throat, she would give his balls a little twist. And when he knew he was going to come, his balls tight to his body, she jerked her mouth from him and dropped to her knees in front of him. Nolan fisted his cock, and using her juices to slide up and down, he came quickly, spraying his cum all over her face and breasts.

Watching her tongue gather some of it into her mouth made his cock fill again. He wasn't sure he could come, but when he stood up, his cock still in his hand, he pulled her to him again and shot the last of himself into her open mouth.

Nolan had to fall back on the table when she moaned or he would have hit the floor when he noticed her fingers deep in her pussy. As she came, Nolan knew that as long as he lived, this was going to be a memory that would be with him forever. He had to lay back on the table again because moving, even to stand up a little, was going to have him falling on his face and hurting them both.

They dressed slowly. He couldn't seem to get enough of touching her. Tasting her skin. Words were quietly spoken and questions that had little meaning were answered just the same way. He knew what they were doing. They were stalling. To leave this room would mean that the world would be there again, and for just the little while they'd been in here, things had been perfect.

"I want you to stop what you're doing." He asked Rylee what she meant. "Stop telling your family that they've barged in on what you were doing. And help them with this. It's a good thing you're doing, but for them, you're souring it by being a big baby."

He supposed he should have been offended by her comment, but his cat even seemed to approve of her assessment of his behavior. When he asked her what she was going to do now, he had to wait until they were out of their little world before she answered him.

"I'll help where I can. I don't know…money has been something that I have no training with. I mean, I know that you've grown up with it, had it all your life, but I haven't, and while I know that this relationship between us is permanent, I need to be my own self and not get lost in you."

"You think I'd do that to you?" She nodded. "I would never try to make you something that you don't want to be,

Rylee. You may not believe this, but I'm falling in love with you."

"I have nothing to say about that. I mean, I've known a few shifters so I know that you tend to fall in love quickly. But I'm not one of you, and I have a responsibility to Shane to make sure he's taken care of too." He thought about telling her what he and Joey had done, but decided now wasn't the time. She wasn't mad at him, but he knew that she was overwhelmed. "And then there is David."

"David Cole?" She nodded. Well, he supposed, now was as good a time as ever. "Don't get mad, but Joey has contacted David's great grandmother about some things that he's said about your sister. Did you know that he's claiming that your sister had affairs while they were married, and that he thinks she died from that, not cancer?"

"I knew. And I made a promise to Shelby that I'd never hurt him so long as she was alive. I don't think she meant to keep me to that promise, but after she got sick, I made sure that it was never brought up again. I didn't want her to change her rules." He smiled. "What have you and Joey done that I might have to kill you both for?"

"So you know, you can't hurt me. But Joey? He's all yours. He got a DNA test from Mrs. Cole. She's going to make her own rules, I think, concerning David." Rylee asked him what sort of rules as they made their way down the hallway again. "I don't know. But Joey said that she's a hoot and that she might have already figured out how to help you two."

"I don't want her help. I just...he should acknowledge his son. Even going so far as to make sure that he has what he needs, should he want to go to college. But I'm not asking for a handout." He knew she was upset, so didn't tell her he was pretty sure there was going to be something coming their way. For all he knew, and he really didn't believe it, there might not be a match anyway. "I'll talk to her if it comes to that. But I just want David to tell Shane he's sorry for what he did to him and his mom, and mean it."

"Do you think that will happen?" She said not without a little help. "So you're going to rough him up a bit, are you?"

"Nah. I'm going to tear his dick off and serve it up to him if he finds that he can't do what I want." She stopped at the doorway to the outside and turned to him. "The school called me. Mr. Simpson wants to have a meeting. I have a feeling that it's not going to go any better with him than it will with David. I was wondering if you'd go with me."

"As a physician or as a cat? Either one will work for me so long as I get to record it." She laughed with him as they moved out into the sunshine.

"Man for now. But the other two if he causes me to get pissy with him. I'm not above going to prison to have this man know he's messed with the wrong girl."

"Not quite. He's messing with the wrong family. And if it's all right with you, I'm going to ask either Chris or Joey to go. They have money to bail us out should it come to that." Nodding, she got into the car with him and he had a sudden thought. "Let's go look at houses."

"Now?" He nodded. "You do know that I don't have any money, right?" He told her that Joey and Micah said they'd help him with the down payment. "Okay, but we should go for something small, don't you think?"

"All right, small it is." He had no idea what he might be getting into, but he reached for Micah to tell him what he was doing. His brother told him that was fine and that he could have a realtor meet him at any house they might look at. *I don't have a clue what we might want, but Rylee is saying small. Just tell her to...how about we swing by and pick up Shane, and you can have her meet us there?*

Sure thing. It's a deal. Micah was giddy. He supposed he wanted his home back, and Nolan could understand that. As he started the car, he thought of how good he felt.

He felt...well, he felt like he'd not felt in a very long time. Alive for one thing, and at peace. Nolan looked at Rylee as he merged into traffic and wondered if it was her or the fact that she'd made him face up to what he'd been doing lately. And how he'd been treating his family. He had told Joey that he'd been a disappointment, but he'd only just realized that it wasn't what they were feeling toward him, but how he felt about himself. He was going to change his attitude and tell his mom he was sorry. And beg the rest of them for forgiveness. Nolan Bentley was turning over a new leaf.

Chapter 6

Rylee wasn't sure this was a good idea. The house—if one could call a sixteen bedroom place simply a house—was bigger than her entire apartment complex, as well as the garage and the yard behind it. She wondered if there would be a pool house or a cook's house out back, and went to the window in the kitchen to see. Yes, there was. A pool house as well as a house for some of the staff, she was told.

"The house has a state of the art security system as well as a guard house, as you might have noticed at the front gate. The fencing around the house and grounds can be electrified if necessary. The pool house, as well as the butler home, is on separate electric should there be a problem in the house, but I assure you, someone would have to be very determined to want to get past the other security around here." Rylee said nothing as they moved to the next room. "The dining room is large enough for a family, or if you wish, these walls can be pushed back and the size triples.

The pocket doors can be hidden away if you entertain on the deck out back."

Rylee tuned her out as she made her way to the living room. Shane had gone up the stairs some time ago, and she knew he was all right. He, of course, had fallen in love with the place and the pool. She hated to tell him that this was way out of their pocket range.

The house was furnished. The previous owners had decided the house was simply too big for them and decided to start fresh when their children had left home. There were no pictures on the walls to give it a homey look, but the furniture was everything she'd want in a home. So long as it was much smaller. As she sat down on the couch to wait for Nolan to tell her they needed to move on, she thought of the conversation she'd had with Chris today. And the entire thing had taken place while she'd been miles away from the woman.

You should know that as of this morning, all your bills, and those of your sister, are paid off. Rylee told her that she needed to not do that and to cancel the payments. *I didn't do it. Mrs. Cole did. She said she had someone looking into a few things, and she realized she should have been doing more for you, Shane, and even Shelby before now.*

I don't want her money any more than I do yours. Chris told her too bad. *Do any of you simply do what someone wants you to do when asked?*

We do, as a matter of fact. But you should also know that as a family, we take care of each other. Rylee huffed. *By the way, there is money in your checking account as well. That I did do. We have…the things at the apartment where you lived. Those weren't yours, were they?*

No. It was all I could afford, and paying for furniture was too difficult along with everything else. Why do you ask? Chris told her. *So you just went in, packed up the household, and had it put in storage for me. Did you ever think to ask me if that was all right?*

I did for a moment, but knew that you were going to be difficult about it. So I just had some...you should know that no one, not even that bastard of a neighbor, knows where you are. I used some very nice witches to go in under cover of magic. Rylee wanted to ask her how that had worked, but wasn't sure she could handle much more today. *He's not...did you know that he has it in his head that you're going to go out with him soon? Actually, it's in his head that you're going to marry him, move into his dirty, nasty house, and keep it for him. The two of you will live off welfare and be as happy as clams together.*

He's a dumbass. When Chris laughed, she did as well. Looking at the stairwell when she heard her name, Rylee left behind her musing to go and see what Shane had found.

"This house is amazing." She told him she thought so as well, but it was too much for their budget. "I figured as much. But you should see this room up here. It's like it was made for me."

They entered the room to the left of the stairs, and all she could do was stare at it. Holy shit, this room really was like her nephew. From the stars on the ceiling to the dark carpet.

Someone had outfitted this room in fantasy. Shane had been fascinated with dragons for some time now, mostly the big ones that showed a great many teeth. But there had been posters in his room that also showed a softer side to them that she had a feeling was more real than not. Lately, she'd wondered if, like vampires and other shifters, there were dragons, and made a mental note to ask someone. She knew Joey had had a vampire friend for a long while, but he'd died recently. But were there dragons? While Shane was showing her the way the closet doors closed up to show the body of a dragon, Nolan joined them.

"Are we leaving? If so, can I take some pictures of this room? Someday I want to have a room like this." Nolan just stared at her, and she had a feeling that something had happened. Shane stopped talking when she stood up.

"What is it?" Nolan just stood there. "Something has happened. Is it your sisters or brothers?"

"We own this house." Shane started whooping it up, but she stared at Nolan as he stood there. "It's why Micah and the rest of them were so happy we were looking at homes. He and the rest of them bought this for us yesterday. I just talked to him."

"Talked or yelled?" He shrugged. "Did Chris have anything to do with the furniture? The reason I'm asking is because this room is too perfect for Shane. Like someone had gotten into his head...can they do that?"

"I don't know, but I would say you're right. I went down the other hall on my way to finding you, and you should see our bedroom. It's...do you like dark colors?" She told him she did in a bedroom. "Well, it's going to be perfect for us then. It looks like something that is deep in a forest and the colors are all from that realm."

She moved out of the room and closed the door. They moved down the hall, looking in each of the rooms as they went. The rooms for the most part were a perfect balance of old and new, and everything was in perfect order. And when they got to the master suite, she could only stare at the size of the bed.

"Yeah, I might have done that." She looked at him. "Come here and tell me what you think of the mattress. Is it too bouncy for you? I like a little bouncy when I fuck you, but you let me know."

"You're serious." He nodded. "This house and everything in it is ours. The pool and the yard? It's all ours?"

"Yes. If you think of something more you want, I'm sure that it'll be there for you." She put her hands over her ears, and he laughed. "I don't think it works that way."

When she told him the mattress was fine, they moved through the rest of the house. When entering the living room again, she noticed that something was different. It took her a few moments to realize that there were pictures on the walls now. Walking up to the largest one near the fireplace, she realized who it was and cried.

"We were taking a walk on one of the many trails around the area, and I was taking a picture of Shane and Shelby. But this man came by and said he'd take one of all of us, and snapped a dozen of them before giving me back my phone. When the phone company shut off our service a few days later, I was glad that I'd gone straight to the store and had a print made of this one." She touched her fingers to the beautiful frame and smiled. "I had enough to get one of those dollar frames to put it in, and it hung in the front room...this is the most beautiful gift that she could have given us."

Nolan came up behind her and held her back to his chest. The picture was only one of a handful of things she had of her sister's. Most of the other things had been sold for food or bills.

"We have to go soon. I was thinking of having Beckman stay here with Shane so he can check out the rest of the house." She turned in his arms and asked him who Beckman was. "The butler. There's a staff too, but I've not met them. He's currently making a list of food that we'll need. He mentioned that the family would be here one night for a house warming party. The date is yet to be set."

"Do you suppose things will ever be normal for us?" He told her that he hoped not. "Yeah, I guess I don't want that either. All right. School, jail, then hospital. I'm saying that now so that we're not surprised when one or both of us ends up in either place."

After telling Shane they'd be back and introducing him to Beckman and two other people that were going to be helping around the house, Rylee and Nolan left. As she was getting in his car, she thought of how much she loved him and had to stop moving or fall on her face when she knew it was true. He asked her if she was all right, and without telling him what she'd just come to realize was true, they went to the school to talk to Simpson.

~~~

Chris was glad they had worked things out. Rylee had brought Nolan back to them, just as she knew she would, and things were looking good for the two of them. As they waited on Simpson and his attorney to show up, she asked them if they liked the house.

"Yes, as you knew we would." She just smiled at Rylee. She was a prickly thing, and Chris just loved her. "Shane is in love with his room. And now that we're going to be getting this crap taken care of, he'll be able to go back to school too. He misses it, believe it or not."

Before Chris could suggest that they put him in another school, the door opened to the office, and five men, including Simpson and his son, walked it. The principal of the school came in behind them, as well as a board member, which happened to be Katie Bentley.

"I don't like this, just so you know." No one said anything to Victor when he sat down complaining. "I think it's a little one-sided to have family here on their side. What if I went on out and got me a friend to be on my side? Then what do you think would happen?"

"You don't have any friends, Victor, we both know that. And should you like to have someone else here, then go right ahead, young man. But I'm not leaving this meeting." Katie sat down and huffed before continuing. "You should be more afraid that my future granddaughter-in-law is going to kick your bottom all over this room if you don't behave yourself. I never liked you anyway, you overbearing pig of a man."

The principal cleared his throat and asked to speak first. "It is my duty to inform all that these proceedings are being recorded. It's school policy that when there is a meeting between two families, things need to be recorded." He sat down. "That being said, I do hope we can resolve this soon. It's disruptive to the other classmates to know this is going on behind the scenes, so to speak."

A sheet of paper was passed around that all of them were required to read and sign, and then the meeting began. Chris had a feeling that Walter Simpson was not going to like the outcome of this meeting, and his dad was going to be even more pissed off. She was going to love every minute of it. The Simpson lawyer started out by handing out paperwork.

"These are copies of the affidavits from fellow students stating that my client was the injured party in this incident. And there are others' statements stating that not only has Mr. Cole provoked this fight, but has been bullying Mr. Simpson for months now." Chris took hers but didn't bother reading it. She knew what it was. A forced document that had no more bearing on the case than anything else that this man had in his little bag of tricks.

"My client and his family are only asking for restitution as well as a formal apology from Mr. Cole stating that he takes full responsibility for his actions and what has happened prior to this one."

"No." Chris was glad now that she'd made it a point to shake each of their hands before this thing started. The lawyer thought this was stupid and felt it was well beneath his expertise. The young man, Walter, was afraid of his father. He'd beaten him three times already since he'd found out that not only was Shane younger than him, but also considerably smaller. The man, Victor, wanted to grind Rylee into the dirt, and had tried to bring a gun in the building, only to be thwarted by the guard at the front door.

This building, like the others that she and Joey owned, was protected. They didn't need any metal detectors, but relied on the magic of the people at the doors as well as what she'd surrounded the place with to keep them safe. She was glad now that they'd used one of their buildings for this farce of a meeting and not the school building, as was suggested.

"I don't understand." The lawyer looked at his client, then back at her. "Perhaps, Mrs. Bentley, you could explain what you mean by *no*. You mean you're not going to pay? You're not going to have your client apologize to mine? There are a lot of things you can say no to, my dear woman. Would you mind narrowing it down so that we can discuss what actions you are going to take?"

"I mean no to them all. My client is not going to pay for any hospital bills. From what I know of your client and his father, there are a great many things going on in that household that shouldn't be, but that's beside the point. There will be no apology either. Not only did my client not do anything wrong or provoke Mr. Simpson, but I have a great many more affidavits than you do that state that Mr. Walter Simpson is a tyrant and a bully." She tossed three thick files on the desk from the pile she had. "These are made without making payments of any kind to the victims of your client. There is also, for each person, a bill from the hospital and an accounting of what was stolen or taken, if you wish, or just plain destroyed by your client when he had turned his anger on them. Did you think that we'd not find the reports filed by the families when you had the sheriff put under investigation as a threat?"

No one said a word. Chris had cautioned Nolan and Rylee to keep quiet, that nothing they could add to this was going to be very helpful. And the losing of temper was going to be her job, not theirs. When Victor stood up, he slammed both hands on the table before leaning over it and her. His smile only made her magic stir up, but didn't piss her off as he'd hoped.

"Now you listen here. You are going to get that golden stick out of your ass and do as I told you to do. Or else." She asked him what that might be. "I'm going to come down on you so hard that you and that stuck-up family of yours is going to be shitting out blood for the rest of your days. I don't care to be pissed off like this."

"Oh, I think you enjoy it a great deal, Victor. As a matter of fact, I know that when you beat your wife, you get off really well with that. And when your son, who is following in your footsteps at being a prick, beats someone that you tell him to, you get your jollies off that as well." She stood up when his face took on the appearance of a man who had been caught with his hand in the cookie jar. "Sit down. And when I speak, you will listen to every word I say."

He did, his ass hitting the chair so hard that she could hear it groaning. He sat there, his eyes glazed over as he was taken deeper under her spell. She didn't care to use this kind of magic, but right now and in the future, he wouldn't be beating his family, and maybe he'd learn a lesson or two from this. Doubtful, but stranger things had happened. Snapping her fingers, she put the rest of the room, with the exception of Rylee and Nolan, into a trancelike state.

"He beats them all." Chris turned to Nolan when she continued. "Not only his wife and daughter, but this boy as well. If Walter doesn't hurt others, like Shane and any of the younger kids whose parents Victor has problems with, Victor makes it harder for him. And he doesn't limit his abuse to just hitting either. Walter spends a great deal of his time locked away in a small room without food or water. It's why Walter does what he does. And you should know that he's sort of glad you are standing up to Victor."

"Why hasn't anyone done anything for them before now?" Before she could answer her, Rylee seemed to figure it out. "Because Victor is a bastard to everyone when he doesn't get his way. You did something to him, didn't you?"

"Yes. I put him and the rest of the people into a sleep-like state. It won't hurt them, but I wanted to talk to the two of you to see what you wanted me to do. I can make him a better person, but that won't last. Magic sometimes isn't as strong as we'd like for it to be, especially when there is so much evilness going for the person. The boy, Walter...he's going to need help if this keeps up. As the future stands for him now, by the time he's twenty-five, he's going to be in prison for murder. And that won't help him at all."

"What sort of things can we do? I mean...short of letting him get by with this?" Chris told Rylee that wasn't her plan either. "Then what? Do we…can we pull him from his family? Maybe, I don't know, bring him under our wing, so to speak? I don't want him hurting Shane anymore, but I don't want him dead either."

"I can suggest to him that he moves out of his house. Gets away from his father. His mother won't take help. While she doesn't enjoy him hurting her, she has had help before and always returns to him. I don't think there is much in the way of help for someone that doesn't want it." Chris sat down and looked at them both. "He needs a guiding hand, but mostly he needs a friend. He has none but those his father sets him up with to teach him the ways of a man."

"Move him out. And he can stay with…there's a house on the property that he can use. I can find him a job, get him…Christ, I hope we don't regret this." Chris assured Nolan that he wouldn't. She promised. "I don't know how you can do this, but we'll help him. As much as we can. But Victor, he pays out of the ass for this."

Chris smiled. "He will. Before the day is out, he's going to pay for his actions. But as before, don't interfere. If you do, everything will go to shit." When both of them agreed, she turned back to Victor. "You have been a terrible person all your life. And you are never going to be any better. That being said, you're going to kick your son out of the house and disown him. You'll never have a thing to do with him again when he tells you that he can't do this anymore. Once you hear those words, you are going to take a swing at your son. Understand?"

As soon as Victor nodded, Chris turned to Walter. The boy had been abused, but not only by his father. His mother, a milksop as she'd heard Katie call her, had been equally horrible to the young man…not with her fists, but with her verbal abuse to him. Chris put her hand on Walter's head and pushed enough of the little confidence he had to the front and made him aware of his actions. Not just now, but things that could go wrong soon if he didn't stand up to his father.

"Tell him you can't be a bully anymore. And when he walks away from you, you're going to go to Nolan Bentley and beg him for forgiveness. It will be the only thing that saves you from prison. If you don't heed my words, Walter, things will go badly for you. Much worse than they were with your father. But in this, like all things, you have free will. It will be up to you what becomes of this." Chris giving him a glimpse of what could happen to him made Walter whimper, but he nodded at her. Tears began to fall on his face when she showed him what could be should he want it. "Tell him as soon as he turns to you, Walter. It will work out if you wish for it to."

As she sat back down, she felt Joey touch her mind. She told him what she'd done, and he asked her if she was all right.

I am. I don't care for using this stuff, but when it helps out someone that really needs it, it's not so bad. He told her that he loved her. *And I do you as well. With all my heart and soul.*

Heath was just by. He said that once we have ten of these horses ready to ship out, he'll have a list of more for us. I think we're going to be doing this for a long time. Chris asked him if he was all right with them taking in horses and other animals and giving them the love and second chance that they needed. *I am. We might have to hire a few more men. I want to make sure that there is enough all the time here so when we can get away, we don't have to worry about the ranch.*

I think I might have someone in mind. He's the boy that hurt Shane. She told him what she'd done and found out. *He's going to need all of our help, and I think this might just be it.*

If you're sure. She told him that she was. *Good. Then make sure that he knows when he fucks up, I will fuck him up.*

He won't. Looking around the room as she told him she'd get back to him, Chris snapped her fingers. The trance left their minds, and she watched Victor as he tried his best to figure out what had happened to him. When he turned to her, she simply smiled at him.

"What are you smiling at, bitch? You think you have the upper hand?" She said nothing, waiting for him to turn to his son. And he would soon. Then she'd have what she needed. "My boy here, he's not done a damned thing wrong, and I'm not going to let you tell the world what you think might have happened." Victor turned to his son when he called to his father.

"I can't." Walter stood up and looked at her, then at Nolan and Rylee. "I'm very sorry for what I did to Shane. More than you can know. But I won't do it again. I can't...I don't want to hurt anyone again."

"You what? You think you can just say that and not have repercussions, boy? You take that back right now or, so help me, I'm going to disown you. You know I will too. I'm a man of my word." Walter stiffened but stood up straighter as he told his dad he was done. Done with it all.

It was over in a matter of seconds. Victor lunged at his son, but when Walter moved, being younger, lighter, and in much better shape, he was able to avoid his father's fists, and even managed to knock him away. But just as everyone was moving to get out of the way, Victor's fist connected solidly with his attorney and he went back, hitting his head twice on the table before falling to the floor. He was dead long before he ever touched the carpet. Chris was still, only moving her lips to tell Nolan to call the police.

It all worked out. The lawyer was a lying piece of shit, and as soon as his death hit the papers, he was going to be in just as much trouble as Victor was for killing him. Walter was free of his family and even the mother and daughter, even though they'd never see it that way, were also free.

As the police were called in, Walter sat in his chair and stared at the table. No one had approached him yet, and the longer he sat there, the more Chris knew he was going to be all right. When he did look up, she could see that he'd come to a major decision and he was going to do just what he needed to become a good man. When he stood up and straightened out his clothing, pressing his hands against his thighs, he let out a long-held breath and sobbed just a little. Making his way to Nolan and Chris, who were talking to the police, he dropped to his knees in front of them.

"I'm not a nice person. I'm not going to lie to you and say that it was all my father's fault. A great deal of it...I'm a grown man and should have taken better care to know that what I was doing was going to come back and bite me in the ass. I'd like to...I need to ask you to...no. I'm going to beg you to forgive me for what I've put you through." He looked up at Rylee. "I cut him because my father said if I didn't hurt him, he was going to castrate me so that I couldn't breed anyone as fucking stupid and lazy as I was. It was wrong, I knew it was. But I thought...."

"You thought what?" Chris started to answer Nolan when it looked as if Walter wasn't going to. "You thought what, young man? You ask for forgiveness, but I want it all from you. You will never lie to me again if you know what's good for you."

"I thought that if I hurt Shane badly enough, he'd turn me in and I could go to prison where I would be safe." Walter broke down then, falling to the floor and sobbing as he continued. "In prison my father couldn't touch me, couldn't hit me no matter what I did to mess up. And I'd not hurt anyone else."

Nolan looked at Chris, and she nodded once and picked up her things and put them in her briefcase. They'd all be fine now. Shane would be upset, she knew, but he'd come around too. Sooner than anyone could have thought.

Chapter 7

Shane knew that this had to be a joke. There was no way they were letting that guy go after all that he'd done to him and the other kids in his school. Looking up at Mrs. Bentley when she said his name, he felt like hitting something and knew he had to get out of the house. Standing up, he was nearly to the door when Mr. Bentley, Howie he'd been told to call him, came in with two fishing poles and a big box.

"Just the boy I wanted to see. Come on, we're going to go and drown some worms." Shane told him he didn't want to, but Howie went on as if he'd not said a word. "I already set us up some nice chairs, and there's this big tree out there that'll keep us cool enough. I had my Katie make us some grub. Not the wormy kind, but real food. Then when we—"

"I really don't want to go fishing. I don't even know how." The man looked crushed and Shane felt horrible, but he needed to be alone, not out with a man that never seemed to shut up. "I'll go with you later. Right now I want to take a walk."

"No. I don't think that's a good idea either." It was the first time in all the days he'd been there that he'd heard the man use such a stern tone in his voice. Shane took a step back, not in fear, he told himself, but in shock. "Now. You've had some news that don't sit well with you, and you and I are going to go and work it off. It's fishing with this old man or chopping wood. And you and I both know that neither of us wants to do that."

Shane was walking behind him to the dock that had been put in only yesterday before he realized what he was doing. He even had a basket of food and a cooler of something to drink in his hands. And Howie was talking about bait.

"I'm a worm man myself. I know there are others that swear by minnows, but I don't see the appeal. Worms are...well, you can cut them in half and they still have enough wiggle in them to attract the most stubborn of fish." He paused to turn and look at him. "You really never been fishing? Not ever?"

"My mom and I lived on a tight budget and there was never the money for a pole, much less a license. Then when she got sick and Aunt Rylee had to come home and help us, there wasn't any more money and there was less time too." He thought about how hard his aunt had worked to keep them going. "I thought a few times we were going to be living in her car. But that got taken too. We really were in a bad way when my mom passed."

"I remember my own mom passing. She was a good woman, but a mite on the quiet side. Never said much, especially things like she loved us or that we meant something to her. Your mom tell you those things?" Shane told him she'd said it all the time. "Yeah, I can tell. I tell my grand boys that too. And Gracie. Loved her from the moment that my son brought her home to meet us. He's gone too, my son. Best son a man could ask for. Miss him more and more of late, what with his sons finding their other halves."

"I don't know where I fit in." It had been on his mind a lot lately, where he was in the grand scheme of things. He knew that Nolan liked him and that all of his brothers did as well, but he wasn't sure what he was supposed to do with this much family. "My aunt said that I should ask what you guys want me to call you. But I think...I should wait, don't you think?"

Howie showed him how to bait his hook. It was kind of gross the way you had to stick the worm so many times to make sure that he was good and stuck on the thing. Then he told him how to cast. It took him a couple of times to get that right, but once his bobber was in the water, he sat on the chair that Howie wasn't using. The man impressed him to no end on how he could simply pick up a conversation like it had been seconds and not nearly an hour later.

"What do you figure you have to wait on? I mean, you thinking that your aunt and my grandson are gonna split up? They won't, let me tell you that. Not ever. And as far as what you are in the grand scheme? I'm thinking of you as my great grandson, just like I do them daughters of Micah's." He told him to watch his bobber, how it was jumping in the water. "That there is the current. Not a fish. Sometimes you might get yourself a nibble or two on it, the little fishes just tasting it to see if it's real, but they don't take much. But you're my family, same as your aunt." And he could jump topics faster than anyone he'd ever met. It took Shane a second or two to realize he'd done it now. From fish nibbles to family again.

"Why?" Shane watched as Howie pulled in his line and then threw it back out again. False alarm, he told him. "Why do you even want me as your family? I mean...I know that you have to take on my aunt...she's gonna marry Nolan. But I'm not even related to any of you, except that I'm Aunt Rylee's nephew."

"And that there is enough. You could be not related to her at all, just some kid she picked up at the store for all I care. She loves you and so do we." That made him think that the man was addled. But then Howie spoke again, and Shane changed his mind. "When my son was killed, that hurt us all. Especially Gracie. She was...she had it in her head that the boys would be better off with us instead of her and she was going to end her own life. Her thinking was that, like you, she wasn't much to us, only someone married to our son. Not anything else but that. So when she told us what she was planning, even going so much as to ask us to remember her fondly, it broke my heart in two."

"She was really thinking that she meant nothing to you?" Howie nodded as he tossed his line back out again. The man was never going to catch anything if he kept that up, to Shane's way of thinking. "But you love her. And her boys, even though they're all grown up, they still need her. I don't think I'll ever not wish my mom was still here."

"Yeah, I bet not. But you do know that your aunt, she feels the same about you." That shocked him. Shane thought that the two of them were doing great. "She feels like she's failed you too. And that boy she saved today, she feels she might not be the best kind of person in his life either."

"Walter?" Howie nodded. "But he'd be the luckiest person in the world to have her in his life. I mean, she and Nolan are all gooey on each other all the time, but they really do seem to fit. I don't think Walter has been around anyone that loved each other like they do. Fists aren't love, they're meanness."

"Exactly. And best yet, that boy? He's gonna be working over at Second Chance too. Did you ever see a nicer ranch than that one?" Shane had wanted to work with the horses, but had never been asked. "I'm betting that before you know it, Joey will be having your butt out there and working them barns too. He's a good — Watch your pole."

Shane had no idea what he was doing but did just what Howie told him. Reeled it in slow but jerk the line. He had to set the hook, whatever that meant. Then he was to let a little out. It took him several tries before he got that down, but the more he reeled the fish in, the harder the thing seemed to fighting him. Then when Howie bent at the waist with the biggest net he'd ever seen, Shane forgot to breathe as he looked at what he'd caught up in it.

"Holy jee-hoes-aphatt. Lookee at what you caught." He did look and could only stare at the thing flopping in the net. "I'm betting this will feed you all for dinner tonight should you take it with you."

"Eat it?" Howie nodded and pulled the fish out of the net and worked at taking the hook out of its mouth. It bled a little, but as soon as it was free, Howie showed him how to hold it in his finger so he could take his picture with it. After he'd taken what seemed like a dozen pictures, Howie asked him what he wanted to do with it.

"You can dress it out. I'll be more'n glad to help you with that. Or you can have it mounted and fixed up so you can put it on your wall. Up to you. Not something I'd do, but that's your first catch and it's a nice one." He looked at the flopping fish and shook his head. "'Course, you could give it a chance to make something of its life. Go back in the water and have some babies of its own. Might even have a couple of them now, but like I said, that's up to you."

Shane might only be fourteen years old, but he knew that the man wasn't just talking about the fish. Walter needed someone to give him a chance, like Shane was getting with his aunt. He leaned down to the fish, picked it up, and looked at the man who had come to mean a great deal to him.

"How do I give it a chance?" He told him to do what came natural to him and the fish. Turning to the water, he dropped the big fish over the side and they both watched as he made his way out to the deeper part of the water. "I'd like to call you Grandda if you don't mind. And I know that Ms. Katie wants me to call her Grandma. Uncle Micah and the rest of them, they told me the same thing. Can I call you that?"

"Would make me about bust with happiness should you do that." Shane watched him wipe a tear from his soft cheeks as he turned to him. "You're a good boy there, Shane. And it'd about make me as proud as you can imagine for you to be calling me Grandda. And to come out here with this old man and fish with him."

"This is a lot more fun than I...I never actually thought about it before. Fishing, I mean." They sat back in their chairs, and Howie pulled two thick sandwiches from the basket and gave him one. "If I keep eating like this, I'm going to be as big as a house, you know."

"Nah. When you sign up for football next year, you're gonna burn it off." That was something else he'd never considered, playing in a sport. "You and me, we're going to get into so much trouble now. You wait and see. And we might even find us a friend in that other young man too. Walter. Walter? What sort of person calls their kid that, I wonder."

For the next several hours, they sat out there in the sunshine and talked. Howie...Grandda caught a fish too, but Shane never caught another one. Which he found to be just fine and dandy, as Grandda told him as they were packing up.

"It's not the fishing and catching, but the drowning the worms and finding out that we kinda like being away from the house. 'Course, we'll have to think of something else when the pond here freezes over. What do you think about hunting? Never did much of it other than to take my gun out to the woods and visit with the animals. You okay with that, son?" Shane thought he could be all right with just about anything so long as this man was with him. "Yes, sir. We are going to raise some hell, you and me. Wait until your grandma hears some of it. But we won't tell her it all. She's a little on the delicate side, she is."

Shane smiled. Katie Bentley was a wonderful person, as was Grace...Grandma, he supposed he could call her now. But he doubted very much that anything the two of them would be doing would be kept from either of them. They had Grandda's number, Shane was sure of it.

~~~

Alta Cole put the phone back in the cradle and smiled. Things were...she was surprised at the way things were going, and that in and of itself was pleasant. She was not usually one for things not going her way, but it seemed that this Rylee McClure was the perfect person to be raising her grandson. Ringing her bell, she waited for Kason to come into the room. When he handed her an envelope, she wondered if the man was ever ruffled. He'd not been since she'd employed him over forty years ago. And truth be known, he was her only friend, too.

"What can you tell me about a man by the name of Bonnifield? He's a big deal in the army, I guess. Something of a prick and a bastard to his men." He frowned at her, but she knew it was more his way of thinking before speaking than him being upset with her asking him such a question. "He has some information that I want, and I want to make sure he's not fucking the girl instead of giving me what I want."

"He would not be having relations with a female." Kason sat down after asking for permission. When he poured them both teas and leaned back, they were no longer employer to employee but man to woman. "He's a good man. Hard when necessary. I do believe it has more to do with his sexual preference than him being that sort of man. I have known of him for some time. Is this...the young man that you've had me put a tail on, this is about him?"

"His aunt, who is raising him, was in his command." Kason nodded, sipping his tea again. "Rylee McClure. You know anything about her other than what I've told you?"

She'd told him everything too. Every morsel she found out now, he would know next. "Nothing much other than what I have heard from the witch that runs the household. Mr. Beckman has been very impressed with the young man, so you might want to know."

"I do. Whenever you find anything, you are to let me know. Even if it's not good news. He and this Simpson person, do you know if they have gotten together? I mean, are they still avoiding each other?" It was something else that impressed her about the couple. Helping the young man was well beyond what she would have done. But after some research and a good deal of money, she'd found out that the young man had suffered as much as anyone had, and she was glad that he'd been taken under their wing.

"Yesterday, as a matter of fact. They didn't seem to know what to do with each other, but Beckman said that they didn't seem to hate each other as he had expected. I do believe that Mr. Howard Bentley had a great deal to do with that. The man has a way about him still." She nodded, thinking about Howie and Katie. Nicest people she had ever known. "When is Master David coming here?"

"Tonight at seven-thirty. Call young Joseph and ask him and his lovely wife to join us, please. I'd like to have them here when he figures out that I'm well aware of it all. I thought about inviting David for dinner too, but then he'd have to bring that woman with him. And those girls...." Alta shuddered. "Have you ever in all your life met a pair of children more like their mother in your life? My goodness, it reminds me of that movie with the girl who rode to the dance in the pumpkin. But they're the two stepsisters, and not worth spit if you ask me."

"I have noticed that the older they get the more they whine. And those voices of theirs. It's like nails down a chalkboard." Kason reached for the scones plate and handed her one, then he took one as well. "I should like to see his face when you tell him what you've found out. Oh, before I forget, I have done as you asked about his bank account. And the hospital was very cooperative about making sure that any and all future billings go to him and not to the family."

"Good. The little bastard might as well make up for lost time. Also, before I forget. I will need to have Jenkins here, as well as Conrad, my attorney. Might as well get all our ducks in a row before he tries to off me tonight." Kason shook his head. "Well, you never know. But you do know as well as I do that what he did with that young wife of his wasn't right. And all for a better piece of the cake. His parents would have been so proud of him. If they weren't already dead, I would be tempted to put them in their grave myself. They did us all wrong by raising him to get whatever he wanted."

"The older he got, I kept thinking that he'd grow out of it, but I do believe that he feels like things are owed to him. Even at his age." She nodded and put her empty cup down. "The Bentleys are panthers. You are aware of that, aren't you?"

"I am. I nearly forgot that...you should invite their...what is he called, their oldest brother?" Kason told her. "Yes, leader. You should invite them as well. Oh, bother and humbug. Invite Nolan and this aunt too. Might as well get them all under one roof when this comes to a head. Might be fun to watch the way she handles this man...Rylee, I mean."

"I should make sure that your homeowner's policy is paid up too." As he stood up, he picked up the tray as well. "I think steaks all around, with maybe a pie. I'm to understand that Rylee has a great weakness for cherry."

"You do that. Make sure that cook knows that we serve only the best tonight. We're going to have some fun." Nodding, he started for the door and she called him back. "Kason, do you think that this boy...do you suppose he'll like me? I had no idea what David was about, and I'd really like for him to like me."

"I believe he will love you. With all his heart. You are a good woman who has a family that...well, you and I both know that they aren't what you would have liked in children. And their offspring have only gotten worse as the years have gone by. Perhaps this young man will be the new blood that makes the other sit up and take notice. I believe...I honestly believe he will be just what we all need. I think...with your permission, I will have the young man come to visit you some time tomorrow. It will be good for you both to get to know each other."

She nodded, and then Kason left the room. Alta was sure that there were going to be fireworks tonight. And more than likely some things were going to be said that she might not want to hear about her own flesh and blood. But Alta was sure as she was sitting there that the sooner this was taken care of, the better off they'd all be. Certainly better for Shane and his aunt. Pulling out the small picture of the boy that Joseph had given her, she stared at his face.

"You're going to be my saving grace, young man." She grinned. "Even if I have to make you do it kicking and screaming the entire way."

Getting up, she made her way to the stairs. Alta wanted to look good tonight. Special things were about to happen, and she wanted to have not just the confidence she might need when it was done, but she wanted David and the rest of them to see her for what she was, not an old woman who lived alone. Smiling, she wondered what Kason would say when she came downstairs with her crown on. The one that she'd been given when she married her late husband.

He'd been royalty. Marcus Michael Cole had been the ninth in line for the crown in his country when he'd met her. And when they'd married, his line had been even longer. As children were brought into the world, his touch with the crown had been put further and further back. After several years of wedding bliss, they knew it was never going to be an issue for them.

When they'd married, his mother had presented her with a crown and scepter as if they were really going to be the king and queen one day. Then she'd taken her aside and spoken candidly with her. Her way with words made Alta, a mere child in comparison to what she was now, feel that she could say anything she wanted so long as it was done with grace and decorum.

"I thought about not allowing him to marry you. Right up until I met you. Then I knew he'd do it no matter how much I fought him or you on it. My boy loves you." She told her that she loved him as well. "Yes, that too helped. But that is not why I wished to speak to you. I wanted you to know you're going to have to move to the Americas. There is...it would be better for my son if he could get out from under his father's rule. Not that my Markus is a bad man, but he likes things his way, and that is, according to him, the only way."

Alta had lived in Thailand most of her life. Her father had been transferred there when she was a child, and now that he was retired, it was their home. But Alta, like her two sisters, had been to the States. Their education had taken place there, as well as visits to the country when shopping needed to be done.

So a few weeks after they'd returned from their honeymoon, they were settled into the house she still lived in, which was bought by his parents, and given a goodly income, as well as all the money he'd had before marrying her. When his parents had passed, all of that and the homes there and other places around the world had come to them as well. Then almost exactly one year later, her Markus had passed away too, leaving her all alone except for Kason and her son. Her son had more use for her money and what it could give him than he had love for her. And his son, as it turned out, was not much different than his father. A greedy little bastard that needed taking down a notch or two.

After taking care of her dress and her hair, Alta waited in the parlor until the guests arrived. She was so impressed with Joseph's wife that she could only hope that the rest of them were just as sweet. And when Micah and his wife arrived with Nolan, Chris, and Shane, she had to grip the back of the seat very hard when Shane put out his hand to shake hers.

"You're my great-grandson, did you know that?"

"Yes, ma'am." He then looked at his aunt before looking back at her.

"You have something to say to me, young man? I like straight-up talk, not beating round the bush."

"You're related to the man that killed my mother." She felt his pain like her own and nodded. "He hurt us, you know. And left us to fend for ourselves. I don't know if you're like him or not, but my aunt said I should give you a chance. Not all worms, Grandda told me, are necessarily from the same patch of dirt."

She nodded, then looked at Rylee before pulling the child into her arms. When he wrapped his arms around her, she had a feeling that they were going to be the best of friends. Shaky ones at first, but things were looking up for her.

"Now then. I'd like to talk about my grandson and the bullshit he pulled on your sister, young lady. Then we're going to discuss how we're going to make his ass pay too."

Rylee stood there for several seconds, and then she laughed. "I think I might like you after all, Mrs. Cole." Alta told her to call her by her first name. "All right then, but you should know that I'm not going to take his shit either. He's on my list."

"Mine too, dear. Mine too." Alta could almost feel sorry for David. Almost. This was going to be so much fun.

Chapter 8

David hadn't been to his grandmother's since he'd married Rebecca, or as he called her when no one was around, Becky. Becky had made it perfectly clear that she didn't care for the old bat any more than he did. But to be summoned this way, and told not to be late, was something he'd been both hoping for and dreading for some time. He was hoping she was going to tell him about the will, but afraid she was going to tell him to straighten up or else. Straightening up wasn't something he thought he could live with.

He'd had his sources in the house. Not very good ones, but he had them. And up until a few weeks ago, he'd been keeping up with his grandmother goings on as much as if he was living in the house with her. Then all the information had dried up. Not just dried up, but the two people he'd had working there had suddenly just stopped contacting him, even about their pay, which he was having more and more difficulty getting to them all the time. His wife had told him that his credit line was no longer available to him. She was next on his list of things to wash his hands of once the old bat was dead and rotting in hell where she belonged.

Kason answered the door when David rang the bell. He was never sure if he should have just walked in or knocked. But since no one told him to just come on in when he'd been there the few times he had, he'd stuck with pushing the bell. Kason asked him to meet the family in the parlor.

"Family?"

Of course, Kason didn't say anything to his query. The man had been treating him as if he were nothing since before his father and mother had died. David had lived with his aunt and uncle until he'd gotten his first check from his mom's estate and had never looked back. He thought that his aunt and uncle had died a few months back, but since he didn't care, he'd never looked into it. They didn't have much anyway, and what little they might have had would have gone to their only child. A girl who had not liked him there as much as he didn't care to be living in her home.

As soon as he walked in the room, he knew something was up. The lawyer was sitting in the chair closest to the fireplace, a place that David had always assumed as his own at his own house. There were three couples there as well, none of which he knew, so he ignored them all. The kid who was apparently with them stared at David like he wanted a piece of him, but David just ignored him in favor of walking to his grandmother. He leaned down to give her a kiss on the cheek, and had to refrain from strangling her when she pushed him away.

"How are you tonight, Grandmother? I had no idea you invited company. I thought this meeting was just going to be the two of us." She started the introductions, and he cut her off. "Shouldn't matter who they are, Grandmother. Not if you wanted to talk to me. Rebecca and I had plans this evening, as I mentioned when you had Carlton call me." He knew what the butlers name was, but liked making him look unimportant to him.

"His name is Kason, as you well know. And you'll listen to me, David, or so help me this will go a good deal worse for you. I'm in no mood for your crap tonight. As I was saying, this is Joseph Bentley and his wife Chris. Reggie and Micah, who is brother to Joseph. This is another brother of theirs, Nolan, and his fiancée Rylee. Rylee McClure." Hearing the name made him think he'd heard it before, but she moved to stand next to the young man. "And this is Shane Cole. Your son."

He stared at the boy, then at his grandmother. Surely there was some mistake. Not that it wasn't his kid, he could see that now, but that she'd figured it out. David looked over at Rylee, just figuring out how he knew her name. She grinned at him, and he felt his world seem to tilt just a little off-kilter.

"I don't have a son, Grandmother. You've met my daughters." For the life of him, he could not think of their names, but moved on as best he could. His mind was circling around the fact that he had to get out of this, and now. "If this is some sort of joke, I'm afraid I don't find it all that funny. I thought we were going to have a nice talk, but I can see now that you think to ambush me with lies and half-truths. I think I'll be going now."

"You leave this house now and I'll have you arrested before you get to the end of the drive. As it is now, you might live a little longer if you just sat down and shut up." He sat on the edge of the seat and looked around the room.

This was going to be death by family. "Now, as I was saying. This is your son, Shane. Shane, I'd like for you to meet the man responsible for you being born. He's not done a whole lot else to be a part of your growing up, but that's going to change now."

"He's not my son. His mother, Shelby, told me that she had affairs when we were married. I told you that. I even showed you the paperwork that she signed off on to prove it." He pulled at the tie around his neck, thinking it felt very noose-like right now. "I should run home and get them. I can have them — what's this?"

The bundle of paperwork that was tossed at him from the man across from him opened, and he could see the copies of the paperwork. Actually, now that he was looking at it, he was pretty sure this was the copies he'd given Shelby a day or two after she'd given birth to her baby.

"As you can see, that's the paperwork that you gave Mrs. Cole when she was still in recovery. The one that you'd had drawn up about her having affairs was never signed by her, as you well know, so the lies you've been spreading about her are false. The one you have had filed away in the courthouse is not only a forgery, but very much against the law. There is also, if you'd care to look at it, a copy of the DNA reports that were given to Shelby when a nurse suggested that she do a test. That was on the day you showed up at the hospital and accused her of all sorts of things that were never true. They rallied around her when you would have had her tossed to the streets."

David didn't even bother looking at them, but let them slide to the floor off his lap. The boy was still staring at him, and David wanted to get up and hit him in the face. But he sat where he was as the lawyer handed him more paperwork that he didn't want to deal with.

"These were written and signed by the staff that day and put away in the event it came that they were needed. There are any number of people that helped your ex-wife that day after you left. It seems that you made quite a show of yourself." He said nothing, but threw the file on the table as the man, Joseph he thought his name was, continued. "Your grandmother was kind enough to have a test done on herself as well. We have narrowed it down that not only is Shane related to you, but quite possibly your son. But you knew that, didn't you?"

"I have no son." He leaned back and looked at his grandmother. "You let these people suck you into this story. The next thing you'll be telling me is that I'm the one that killed Shelby. Well, I know for a fact that she died from cancer, and the last I looked, I can't give her that."

"No, but you did make it so that she couldn't get the care she needed, didn't you, asshat?" He knew that Rylee was pissed at him. And knew there was nothing at all she could do about it. They might be able to prove that Shane was his son, but he could just say Shelby had never told him it was his. It might work. "Why did you sell the house, David? Why did she never see any of that money? She was, under law, entitled to half of the sale of it. It would have gone a long way into making things better for her. Certainly for her son, who still needs his mom."

"Half? For having affairs during the time that I trusted her? I don't think so." This time Conrad, his grandmother's attorney, stood up and handed him a file. "More paperwork? What do you think this is going to do? I won't need to read it to know that she all but admitted to having affairs that day. It's why I was so angry." He had to make them believe he was the injured party in all of this. He felt he was, really. Injured that it had come back to haunt him.

"You were angry that she wouldn't sign off on the statement you brought to her in the hospital. No other reason than that. Screaming and yelling at her as if she were nothing to you. But you should know, David, even back then, the hospital had cameras with sound in each room. And since you made such a big commotion about this, they kept that recording all this time in the event that someone — and in this case, Joey here did — came back to ask questions. To find out if anything could be done to prove not only was Shane your son, but that Shelby had been entitled to more than you ever gave her in the form of help." Conrad nodded to the file in his hand. "That's a transcript, as well as a link you can go to and download it to see it. I have sent copies to the newspaper, too, as well as your lovely current wife."

He opened the file now; the sweat going down his back was making him sticky and a little nauseous. This couldn't be happening to him, he kept thinking. What would happen to his money and inheritance? What of his grandmother's money? The more he read over the words that had spilled from his mouth, the more he realized what a fool he'd been with this. There should have been a plan in place, something he could fall back on. David always had a plan. He had to get out of there, if for no other reason than to try and fix this with Rebecca.

Standing again, he felt the hair on his arms and neck stand up as the man with Rylee got up. He was sure he'd been mistaken about the low growl that had come from him, but when he took a step toward him, David was sure his face shifted and changed into a large black panther before righting itself back to a man. David fell back rather than sat this time. He looked over at his grandmother.

"Grandmother, you can't let them treat me this way. I'm your only remaining heir." He glanced at his son and felt his balls tighten up. "There is just no proof this kid is mine. Even DNA tests aren't one hundred percent accurate. And even if they were, he's not fit to be a Cole. Just look at him."

"I have. And I've had a long talk with him as well. His mother, rest her soul, was a good woman who told him daily that despite your treatment of her and him, she was glad that he was born of your union. I can't imagine what she went through to try and make ends meet after what you did to them." Grandmother moved to stand next to Shane. "Did you know that had his mother had the assurances from you that *you* promised her in writing that she'd get if she divorced you, that she might have lived a long and very happy life? And no matter what, you made it so that not only did you not pay her one dime in compensation, but you even made it so every time there was a little money to be had by them, you ate it up in lawyer fees and court costs. As it was, you cut it short by denying her even the basic help she deserved, like security and medical insurance. Also, when you took the house and took her to court every time you heard about a windfall, it just added more and more stress on her already depleting body. How could you, David? How could you just abandon your own blood?"

"Why am I the bad guy in all of this? I mean, like I said, I didn't give her cancer. And even if I could have afforded to give her every little thing she wanted, I didn't want to take away from my new wife and children." He tried to look like a man who was beaten by this. But Rylee snorted at him and the other woman, the one with Micah, just laughed. "You should know your place, too, young woman.

I'm a Cole, and we don't like underlings making us look bad."

"Underlings? Really? Well, I hate to burst your bubble, dickweed, but Micah and his family have had money since well before you were a spark in your father's eyes. And not to mention, my place, as you called it, is right here, with my family. The one that you didn't even care enough about to see if he needed anything when his mom died." She pointed to Rylee, who was still staring at him, and the man who was standing beside her. "Do you know what she said when she found out that this was going to happen tonight? She said she didn't want anything from you."

"Smart woman, since she's not getting anything from me." He looked at his grandmother. "Why am I here? The woman is dead. Okay, we get it, boo hoo for them. But this has nothing to do with you and me." Grandmother just shook her head at him. "Do you think that, I don't know, we can somehow raise her from the dead and make things all better for him? Well, I hate to burst your bubble, but it doesn't work that way."

"I've taken your inheritance from you." He started to stand up, but he wasn't sure that his legs could hold him. "Not to mention you've paid off a few of your ex-wife's outstanding bills. Hospital, as well as a few things that were never covered when Shelby died. You should be ashamed of yourself, David."

He looked at Rylee, his anger no longer simmering but boiling over the pan and into the hot flame. "You did this. I don't care what you told them, but you are trying to ruin me with your lies and stories. You came sniffing around to get a few bucks off me, and now you've got yourself all set up nicely. Well, I got news for you, it won't work. I'm not a sap, and I won't be paying any more shit for you."

"I had nothing to do with this. You did this to yourself when you fucked my sister, and I don't mean just with your dick." When she stood up, he felt his balls tighten to his body. He'd heard of her, and that was enough. She was one tough, angry bitch. "Believe it or not, I'm not going to hurt you physically. I'm not...you don't mean enough to me to want to hurt you. What you did, what you did to your son and wife? Those are things you're going to have to live with, not me."

"I don't give a shit about what you think I might have done to them. I did what was necessary to make my life better. There wasn't much in the way of perks for me to stay with your sister. And to have a son would have weighed me down in a way that you cannot imagine. I needed to be free to pursue things that I wanted. Do things that made me happy. Why is that a crime?" He felt himself get braver after she said that she'd not hurt him. When he stood up, she backed from him, but the man, Nolan, stood still. "She was boring, if you want to know the truth. I wanted...I wanted a life. Not stuck in a marriage centered around a kid that I would have to take care of should she finally be able to work. I wasn't...it's not in my blood to have a job, and there wasn't enough money with her to make it worth my while. And when she got herself in trouble with that brat, I decided that enough was enough."

"And the children you have now, with your current wife, they didn't cramp your style?" They had, and he told her so. "I see. So in order for things to be the way you want them, you'll just get rid of the extra baggage and move on."

"Why not? It's not like Becky needs me to pay her any kind of support...not like your sister wanted. And since I was smart enough to not sign the pre-nup she kept shoving in my face, I will get to go on living in a lifestyle that I've grown to like, despite the fact that Grandmother thinks that taking my money from me is going to work. I might even ask Becky for more since she has it all and Grandmother is a selfish bitch. And when I find me a nice little thing, with more money than brains, I'll get myself another wife. But there will be no more children to have to be screaming about their needs. This time I've taken precautions in the baby making department." He grinned when he thought of the little snipping he'd had done. "The next wife will be just that, a wife until someone better comes along."

"David?" He turned slowly when he heard her voice. Looking at Becky, who was standing in the doorway with her father and mother, he knew that he'd been set up for a great fall. And there were witnesses to it. The fucking butler, Kason, was smiling at him like he knew something that he didn't. "What do you mean, until something better comes along? You said that you would love me for all time. What is the meaning of this?"

"Yes. That's something I'd like to know as well." Mr. Poser came into the room. Becky's father was no one he wanted to ever fuck with, and now he had. And from the look on his face, David knew that pre-nup or not, he was royally fucked.

~~~

Rylee was sort of...she wasn't sure what she was feeling right now, but not good was a little of it. David had really been a bastard, just as her sister had said. Not that she'd not believed her, but to see him, hear his words...it was just sickening. But she was pretty sure he was getting his comeuppance.

"Do you suppose Mr. Poser will do what he says to him? To David, I mean. Do you suppose he'll follow through on suing him?" Rylee looked over at Nolan and smiled when he continued. "He was pretty pissed. I mean, my cat wanted to tear him apart when he said those things about my son, but hell, that man is more vicious than me."

"Your son?" He grinned at her. "I don't know if that's a good idea right now. He's having some…Shane is having a sort of crisis right now. This thing with David, I think it was good that he could hear what kind of person he is, but to have your own blood say those words in front of you…damn it, I want to go and tear him up too."

"He's going to be great. Shane has a good head on his shoulders, and he seems to know what he is about. And we talked. Shane and I had a long talk the other day, and we're coming to terms with each other. I love the kid." Rylee turned slightly and looked at Shane, who had a set of headphones in his ears as he stared at the small computer in his lap. She looked at Nolan and asked him what they had talked about. "Manly stuff, for one thing. He's calling Mom 'Grandma,' and he's calling my grandparents that as well. Grandda is in love with him too, and cannot wait to go fishing with him again. Did you know that he caught a huge fish?"

"I did. He sent me a picture. You talked to him about you calling him your son?" Nolan grinned and shook his head. "What do I have to do to get a straight answer out of you?"

"Oh, I can think of any number of things you can do to me. But for this, I'll simply tell you." He laughed again. "I asked him if I could adopt him as my son. Of course, you'll have to adopt him first. That's the only way I can have him as my son. You don't want to be his aunt living with his dad, do you?"

"Maybe we'll just go back to that apartment that you first found us in and cut you out altogether." He looked wounded and she laughed. "I don't think that would work either. Shane really likes his new room. And I have to thank your mom, too. Did you know she got him into the private school without going by way of the waiting list?"

"She said she had pulled some strings." He glanced at her as he drove. "She has a scary amount of strings she can pull. Grandma as well. Grandda told me once that she could call the president right up if it suited her needs, and he'd not be the least bit surprised if the army was on our front porch should she need them."

That didn't surprise her at all. She'd even gotten a call from her old captain from the service the other day. He'd told her that she could do them and the service a great deal of good should she want to come and work for them. As a recruiter, not on the front line again. He'd explained to her that according to Katie Bentley, she was needed at home, not there. He went on to tell her to make that woman happy at all costs, to never make her mad, and to try and find the bodies she'd buried of those that had done all the above. Rylee had thought he was kidding, but now wasn't so sure. She decided to tell Nolan what she'd been thinking about for a few days now.

"I don't know what to do with my life. I mean now that I've met you and I'm not in a constant panic about what to do to make the next rent or how to buy food." Nolan asked her what she meant. "I don't know. I was army all the way for so long that I don't think I know anything else. Then there is the fact that with Shane not needing me so much with this new school, I'm at a loss for what do to."

"Okay, first, why do you think that he won't need you as much? That kid will need you more and more as he gets older. I do my mom. She's my world. She scares me, but she's there for me. And secondly, I need someone to help me with all this stuff I have going on." She asked him what stuff. "When I purchased the building for the homeless shelter, I kind of took on a few more buildings too. One of which, as you know, is a warehouse. The others — there are nineteen of them total — are in need of work and businesses at the end of five years or the city takes them back."

"Take them back why?" He told her. "So, if you don't make some improvements and have a business in a building that you own, they can just come in and take it back from you? No questions asked, just take? That's bullshit."

"Yeah, well, at the time, I thought it was a wonderful idea." He frowned, and she wondered what was going on now. "I want to turn a few of them into apartments. Not like the one that Chris and Joey have, but something like studio places for people to just live. Maybe…I was thinking of something like a studio apartment where they can work should they want to. Also, I wanted to see about an antique place. Mom said there is one in the next town over that does a good business, but the couple who own it are wanting to sell their inventory and convert the place back into their home. I thought…I was going to see about buying it from them."

"Consignment. You could take it on consignment for a while. And I know this guy who has some old crap, too, that he wants to get out of his house." She was warming to the idea of being a person in business for herself…well, the two of them in business for themselves. "He's a vampire of considerable age, and when I talked to him at Shelby's funeral, he was telling me he wants to clean house."

Her mind was working over the idea of getting in touch with Barron. He'd always been there for her when she'd needed him. But with this thing with money and such, she'd felt bad enough that he'd bailed her out of something when she'd been hurt, she didn't want to bring him in on that too. He would have just paid everything off and given her enough money to live on for the rest of her life. Sounded good, she supposed, but it wasn't her style.

"So, you'd be willing to help me out with this stuff? I have my practice too. And while I'm on call, you might have to take on a business of ours by yourself." She was nodding and thinking about what she wanted to do for this to work. "You really want to do this, don't you?"

"I really do. And I don't know which building you were talking about to convert into a shop, but I'm sure we can make it work out." He just shook his head at her. "You know, I think I might need to start on this tonight instead of running in the woods behind the house with you."

"Oh no, you don't. I have been looking forward to this all day, and you are not taking this from me now." She just grinned. "I might have forgotten to mention that Shane knows what I am. He's sort of okay with it, but he doesn't want me to shift around him, not yet anyway."

She could understand that. The few times that Nolan had shifted in front of her, it had been sexy. But with Shane, it was something new. And scary new to him. As they drove the rest of the way home in silence, Rylee wondered what they were going to do now as a family.

Beckman met them at the door as soon as they came up on the large deck. He didn't look to be stressed, but he did have a look on his face that made her think he'd been pinched. Smiling at him when Nolan asked him if everything was all right, the gentlemen only shook his head.

"There is a person here. A vampire. He wishes to have a conversation with the lady of the house." He looked at

124

her. "He said that you are his little lady, and that he only just heard of your finding a mate."

"Can we see him in the living room?" Nolan and Beckman both shook their heads at her. "Okay, he's the friend I was telling you about earlier, and if he's not welcome in this house, I'm not —"

Nolan put his hand gently over her mouth, and then he kissed her nose. "He can't come in until you invite him. And there has to be rules too. Beckman is a witch, in case I forgot to mention that." Shane whooped with excitement, and Nolan looked at him with a cocked brow before continuing with her. "You have to invite him in and tell him that no one, especially the witches that are here, can be his meals. Witches and vampires do not usually get along."

"Will you turn him into a frog, Mr. Beckman?" Smiling at her nephew, Beckman took him into the kitchen as the two of them stood there.

As they moved to the front of the house, having come in from the kitchen, Nolan asked her about her friend.

"His name is simply Barron. He told me once that if he had a last name, he'd long since forgotten it." She moved to open the door and looked at Nolan. "He's a bit odd. More so than you are. But I think that his is more due to the fact that he's eccentric rather than him just being odd."

From the other side of the door, she heard Barron tell her he heard her, and she opened the door to find him not one day older looking and just as flamboyant as he'd ever been. "Hello, my little chickadee. How are you faring now that you have yourself a nice mate?"

Chapter 9

Barron simply loved her mate and the young man, her nephew. When he'd first met the younger woman, she'd been in her cups and he'd thought to take advantage of her. But she delighted him so thoroughly that he hadn't the will to harm her. But he drank from her. It was their pact. Should she ever need him she needed only to call to him. Which, it seemed, she no longer did. That both saddened him and made him very proud to know her.

"Nolan and I are going to open an antique shop. I was wondering if you still had some things you wanted to get rid of cheaply." He smiled at the thought of her as a merchant. "I'm not sure how much we can pay you, but I think we can make it work."

"I can put it in there for now, and if you sell it, you can pay me. I have no need for the money." He didn't either. Barron had been around for a very long time, and money had lost all of its appeal to him. "I have come here on a very important matter, however. I should like to know if you have the time to listen to me."

He knew they had had plans for tonight. Even hated to intrude on them, but he needed her, as she was his last hope. Nolan said he'd be back and left them alone. To have a panther, even one as newly mated as they were, to leave a man alone with his mate spoke volumes for the man and his trust of his mate.

"Is it about your daughter?" He'd told her everything one night. It had been a mistake, he'd thought at the time. But it had turned out to be the best thing he'd ever done. She had more information about him than other vampires he had known for centuries, and she had never told anyone. This he knew to be a fact. "Did you find her?"

"I have. But to say that she is upset with me still would be grossly understated. She blames me for her lot in life, and I find I cannot really blame her. It's not as if I didn't love her, but when her mother died...it took more out of me than I had for the child. So when I had to go and recover...well, as I have told you before. Leaving her in the hands of my brother was a mistake. This I know now." Barron had told her this story before. "She will not even let me talk to her. Has not allowed me to come to her home, and...and I have heard she has her own mate now, and there is a child."

"You have a grandchild." He grinned and nodded. "Congratulations. Have you seen it yet? What is it? Boy or girl?"

"A young man. He is older than the young man in the kitchen. Your nephew, I believe?" She nodded, and he could see the happiness on her face. "My grandson is nearing his age of turning. To becoming a full vampire. And I would wish that you talk to her for me. Not intercede on my part, but to see if she will see me, and soon. I should like to make sure she has what she needs, and I would like to make sure that what I have been told about my grandson is true."

"And what is it you think she might need? Besides you in her life? This grandson, what might he need that you can give him after being out of his life for so long? I don't mean to be a bitch about this, but it has been a very long time, Barron." Barron wanted to tell her everything, and knew in that moment he more than likely would have to before she would help him. He looked at her when she cleared her throat. "You've had her investigated. What is it you're not telling me?"

"You were always too smart for your own good, my child." He got up to sit near her. Not close enough to touch—he knew the ways of mates—but to hand her a picture he'd had taken of the boy. "His name is Dennis Barron Richards. I think she likes me a little with that name, but he is...because her mother was not a vampire when Constance was born, there have been...complications for Constance's child. He will not live a long and fruitful life, as I have been told by someone. I wish for her to allow me to help him."

"He's dying. Or he will die, right?" Barron nodded sadly. It hurt him that his wife and longtime lover had gotten with child before he'd thought to convert her. Then when he had, there were things that had gotten them...well, gotten her into trouble. She was protective of him, and that had gotten her killed one day when he'd been in his slumber. Connie was...had been a day walker...someone who could stand the sun yet be a vampire too...a trait that was coming to his grandson because his mother was not a full blood either. "What can you do to help him? Change him?"

"Yes. If he is not converted before he reaches his time, then he will surely die. His father is a pureblood as I am, but I'm older. More powerful in the simple fact that with age, considerable magic comes to me." He got up to pace. "You know what a day walker is, am I correct? But do you know they have powers within them that even their maker does not have? My Connie had such powers, but they were...when she was angry or stressed because of the actions of others, she would shift. There was no control over it for her, or, I think, she never cared to have control over it. Back in those days, it was safer for us to be...less gentle with humans than we are now. More...I guess you could say we were monsters then, and have, in my opinion, come a long way to change that. So when she did it at the wrong time, she was killed."

"And your grandson, he does this too?" Barron shook his head. "Then what is it you feel you can heal him from?"

He'd known that it would come to this. Not that she'd demand to know answers, but he knew her well enough that she would not just go blindly into something without first making sure she had all the information. This, even helping him, would be no different.

"He has no fangs, and because of what he is, if he does not have them, he will not survive." She asked him how that was possible. "He has the teeth of a human, something that has been passed to him from his grandmother through his mother. I should like to...if I do not help him with a conversion soon, he will starve to death after only a short time once he is changed."

He watched her face. Barron knew that she didn't want to help him. He wasn't sure he really blamed her either. But it was written on her face. He'd realized a long time ago she would not be one to win at poker, because her face told it all. It was difficult enough for him to come here and ask. He could not imagine having to go into a den of vampires she did not know to convince one of them to let another vamp...Christ, what was he even doing here? He decided he was going to go. As he was moving to the door, she said his name softly and he turned to her before speaking his heart, something he did so seldom that it tore deeply into his chest.

"This was wrong of me. To come here and impose on you and your mate. Especially since you are newly mated and of no need of problems that are not your own. I am truly sorry, love. I am." He opened the door when she said his name again. "I will have those things delivered to you as soon as—"

"Shut the fuck up." He turned to her, both impressed and a little pissed that she should shout at him so. "Damn it all to hell, but you do go on when you have to be right, don't you? Where is this grandson and how do I contact him?"

It took him several seconds to realize what she was asking him, and a few more to find a place to sit before he fell over. She was...she was impressive in her ability to fool him. And he also had to think that her mate might be in for more than he'd known from this woman.

"You wish to do this? You do know that he is a vampire and that as such, his family is as well. And being a friend of mine, it will not...." He looked at her face and noticed the cocked brow at him. "Yes. I will get you the address. It is not far from here."

After Barron sat back down after going to his home to get the information she'd need, her mate returned. The man was very protective of his mate, and had more than likely known she was distressed about this.

Barron told the both of them all he knew about what had happened and how he knew what was going to happen when he changed the boy. Soon, the younger man, Shane, came into the room and joined them. After shaking his hand during the introductions, Barron had a sudden thought as to how he could return the favor for what she was doing for him. He would have to give it some thought, but now that the idea had formed, he was brimming with the need to make it happen. He would help the young man in a way that only he could. A little part of him would protect the boy no matter the time of day or the need. It was the least he could do after she was willing to help him like this.

As he left the house of his now good friends, he put his hand on the boy's shoulder and gave him a little of himself. The rest, he knew, would come to him soon, more in the way of monetary gain, but for now this was going to have to do. The child would go far in his life, and Barron wanted to be a part of it. Would be a part of it. Leaving, Barron felt better than he had in weeks, centuries really.

~~~

Rylee made the call as soon as Barron left them. She knew a little more about his kind than she had before, but it didn't give her any more of a good feeling about what she was going to be doing. The man who answered the phone was polite but not very helpful.

"I will give the lady of the house the message that you called." She told him that it wasn't going to work for her. "I beg your pardon?"

"You will need to have her come to the phone now. It's a matter of life or death." The connection was closed, and she growled out her frustrations. But as she turned to tell Nolan she was going there, Beckman and the most...well, colorful did not even come close to describing the woman who was standing there with him.

"My lady. This is Myra. She is the royal witch to the queen." She asked him who the queen might be; just kidding really, but he nodded and smiled. "That would be my queen, Lady Chris. Your sister-in-law."

"I see." She sat down and felt her body tingle. "Why is...is there a reason that the royal witch Myra is here in my living room? I mean, is she...why are you here?"

"You are so adorable. I'm here because you are set on a quest that I wish to help you with. Barron and I have been...well, not friends, as you are to him, but we had a thing some time ago. He is a wonderful lover and at—" Rylee raised her hand and Myra laughed. "Yes. That is for another time. But I am here to help you, should you like for me to. While it will be up to you, it would make me...I want to help our friend as well."

"What's it going to cost me?" Myra tisked at her, and Beckman looked shocked. "There is nothing in this world for free, Myra. Even you have to know that. Chris is a really wonderful person, as is Reggie, but the fact that you're here and not them makes me think you haven't told them you're going to help. Why is that?"

"You are brilliant, aren't you? But to answer your question, I am here because it is personal to me. You can and will do this on your own should you want, but with my help, my...magic, it will go easier for you. And a good deal safer for you." She asked her why she was going to need safety. "Because the man you seek is a man that I do as well. Ansel Vegas is a man who, for all appearances, is a good one, when I know for a fact that he is not. I should like to confront him on a couple of things, that's all."

"No one, no matter what they say, has always been a good person. You'll have to do better than that." Rylee reached for Nolan and hit a wall. "Are you keeping Nolan from coming to me?"

"I am." Myra sat down on the chair and that was when Rylee noticed the change in her color. The dress as well as her hair and shoes were all one color. A green so bright she was sure that neon would not have even come close to matching it. "I should like to make you aware of a few things about this house that you do not...that you should know. First I would like to start with the room your nephew is in. It is—"

"If you hurt him, I will hunt you down and tear you apart. I'm not a shifter like the rest of them, but I will die trying should you touch him." Myra nodded and smiled. "I should just let you finish, right?"

"Yes. The room he is in, it is magical. All of it. But it is the dragon on the door of his closet that you should be made most aware of. It is real." She wondered for a second if she meant the doors were real or.... Rylee asked her to explain. "You have it right. The dragon is real. It is his protector. And soon, on his next birthday, the dragon will move to his body and mind, and he will keep him safe even out of the room. He must be of an age where he can make decisions. While he can now, there are guidelines even I must follow."

"Why? Is something going to happen to him that he'll need the extra protection?" Myra told her there was always need for extra protection. "You know what I mean. Don't be obtuse."

"Not that I am aware of. He will live a somewhat normal life. But the dragon will be there should he need him. And he might." Rylee wasn't sure if she believed her or not, but asked about the rest of the house. "The house is also protected, as you have found out tonight when you needed to invite your young vampire in."

"Young vampire?" Myra nodded and ran her hand over her hair to her waistline, and Rylee was distracted by the color change for a moment. She looked at the other woman and wondered if she'd done that on purpose. Her smile made Rylee think she was reading her mind as well. "Barron is very old, thousands of years old. How do you get off calling him young?"

"To me, he is." Rylee felt her mouth dry, and her body seemed to do a hard reboot. Barron was young compared to her. That looped in her head for a few minutes as she tried to get her mind to focus on anything else but that. "You will be all right, Rylee Dean. And I will be glad to see you blossom."

"I don't want you to...what do you mean you want to help by keeping me safe? I'm just going to talk to this woman and her son and see what I can do to save his life." Myra shook her head. "You'll have to do better than that. I'm not a mind reader like the rest of you are."

"But you are. As is Nolan and young Shane. Do you not remember Chris telling you that you are as they all were? I do believe she said that to you the very first day she met you." Rylee remembered something like that. She'd said Rylee was like them but for the shifting part. "See, you knew that all along. There are a few...Chris for one, me for another...that you will not be able to read. We have given you this gift and as such, we are out of your bounds."

"Yeah, so I can read minds. Not doing me a lot of good right now, is it? And don't think I didn't see how you shifted that around to something else when I asked you about why you wanted to go with me." Myra stared at her for several seconds before she threw back her head and laughed. Rylee wasn't sure what was so funny, but waited for her to regain control. When she looked at her then, her game face on, Rylee knew that something was up.

"Ansel will kill you if given the chance. Not that day, but...he will not be happy that someone has deemed him unfit to care for the boy and his mother. He is...how should I say...? He is not a nice person to deal with, not even for those that he has taken under his protection." Rylee watched her face to see if she was telling her the truth, but had a feeling not only was she telling her a fact, but there was more to it than that. "There is. Should you like to know?"

"I think so." Myra nodded but said nothing. Which, she supposed, was a good thing, as Rylee was still trying her best not to freak the fuck out. "This magic I have from being a Bentley...what is it, and how do I use it?"

"You just reach out as you do when speaking to one of the others, but instead of speaking, you listen. It will take you some time to get used to doing it without hurting them. Digging too deeply into their head will harm the other, as it will you. And if they try to block you, which stronger people can, you could cause death to you both." Myra waved her hand, and a book appeared. "This I can lend to you. It is very important to your family that no one but you and perhaps young Shane read this. As for your powers, you can also bring smaller things to you for now, larger as you gain more control. And move quickly."

"Quickly, as in I can move from someplace here to there fast." Myra nodded, and again she thought there was more to it than that. "And this book, when I read it, I'll understand what I can do."

"You will." Rylee nodded, but didn't touch the book now lying on the coffee table between them. "You're not trusting, are you? I should have known that about you. I have been watching over you since you were brought here. You will learn to relax some now."

"No, I'm not very trusting, and if I do get to the point where I'm a little more lax in that, I hope someone will hit me. I don't want anything to happen to any of those I love. And if you've been in my mind, you know that too." Rylee thought about the thing with Barron. "Why will he try to kill me, this Ansel person?"

"He does not like humans." Fair enough, but not a good reason to kill her. "And you will have something he wants."

"And what do I have that an old vampire wants? This magic? I don't think so. He more than likely has more than me." She said that he did in some things. "Then what is it?"

"You, my dear, have Barron." She asked her what she meant. "He is your friend and your best-kept secret. The man loves you as his child, and more than that, he has shared with you what he has."

"Magic." Myra only shrugged. "Do you suppose we can cut the bullshit with the vague answers and questions? Just tell me what the fuck you're doing here, and what Barron has given me."

When she stood up, Rylee did as well. But when she dropped to the floor on one knee, Rylee reached for a gun that she no longer carried and hadn't for some time. When Chris appeared in the room with two men she'd never seen before, her body seemed to go into defense mode, and she looked around for something to use as a weapon.

"She can be a pain in the ass, can't she?" Chris snapped her fingers and the men moved to the doors, but never left them. "They know a vampire was here. And they're a little nervous around Myra still."

The woman on bent knee laughed but didn't rise, not until Chris told her too. When they were all seated, Nolan and Beckman came in. The butler was pushing a tea trolley with a large pitcher, as well as the biggest plate of cookies and other treats she'd ever seen. But instead of giving her a cup of the brew, he handed her a large glass of what turned out to be juice. She asked him what it was.

"My own special blend of fresh fruit. You will need to drink some daily once you start to use your magic." When Shane joined them then, he was handed the same juice and was told to drink it first. He drank it down before turning to her.

"I can do some weird crap now." She asked him what. Instead of answering her, he put out his hand and three cookies came to him. "I can move books too. And make my bed. My room, by the way, is now spotless. I didn't do that, but I think something did."

"That would be the house." Beckman handed her a plate of cookies as he continued. "It is so that there is no need for more people within the walls than necessary. It will keep you safe. The ones that are here now, they are of my choosing and will not harm you or they will die. Will you be joining us for dinner, my queen?"

"Wait, wait, wait. They will die. Just like that, you can say that." He nodded and handed a plate of cookies to Myra, who was now dressed from head to toe in paisley. And the trolley with the cookies on it...there looked to be just as many as there had been when he rolled it in. She looked over at Nolan when he laughed.

"Welcome to the Bentley family, my love. Where nothing is as it seems, and if you don't like it, just think of something different." She didn't think he was the least bit funny and told him so. "If you don't laugh about it, you'll go insane. Trust me. Micah had to come to terms with it too. But we can set up rules, as he's done. No one messes with his bedroom. The making of the bed is fine, but nothing else. And his office is off-limits altogether."

She wanted to tell them that all of it was off-limits, but one look at Chris changed her mind. The smallest shake of her head had Rylee thinking she'd have a long talk with her later. When Shane picked up the book that Myra had given her and asked to be excused until dinner, she let him go. Things were…it was hard enough for her to understand this crap. She had no idea what he was going to do with it. But then, with Shane, he more than likely thought it was neat and he could go with it.

The phone ringing beside her had her looking around. Myra told her to answer it, but all Rylee could think about was there had not been a phone there before. At her second prompting to answer it, she picked it up.

"My name is Constance Vegas. You called here earlier and spoke to my butler. He didn't get a name but…." Rylee looked at Myra, who smiled. "I…I don't know why I am, but I had the sudden urge to call you. What is this about?"

"I'd like to see you. Soon. Now if you can manage it." Constance said nothing. "It really is a matter of life and death. That of your son, actually. I have someone that can save his life."

"Are you threatening us?" Rylee told her that she had information that she might not have. "You're that friend of my dad's, aren't you? The woman…the one he talked about when he visited me? Rylee something…he said you were his only friend."

"Yes. He's my friend, and yes, he did come to see me about you. Tonight as a matter of fact. I need to…. It's really important that I talk to you about your son, Dennis." She asked her what it was. "I would like to come and see you. With some friends that can help him."

"You mean my father. I don't have anything to do with him anymore. We had a falling out." Rylee knew about that and the why of it. "He's not…he's not really welcome here."

"He is the only one that can save his life." Rylee looked at Myra and then reached out to Constance to see about reading her mind. She saw she was afraid, but not of her. She was afraid of her husband…and not just that, she worried for her son as well. "Barron thinks your son will die because he was born without the ability to have fangs. When he converts on his birthday, he will be dead within a few days. His inability to feed will starve him. You believe me or not, but Barron said that once he converts, there will be no helping him."

"And you know this how?" There was a touch of fear now, and Rylee thought of what Barron had told her and showed Constance by projecting the information to her mind. Or at least she hoped she was. When the woman sobbed, Rylee thought perhaps she'd hurt her, but the woman started to cry. "I'm going to check that out. I'll…if you're lying to me, I will hunt you down, Rylee. This is not something you to do a vampire, threaten their child unnecessarily."

"You don't threaten a human either with that. I'll await your call. I'm going to help you if you'll let me, but there will be rules. One of which is you meet me during the day. I know you can do that." Constance said she'd see and hung up. Rylee turned to the room. "I'd very much like for you all to go away now. I know I'm being really rude, but I'm so overwhelmed right now that all I can think about is a hot bath and a warm body wrapped around me."

They just disappeared, save Nolan. Not only the other people, but the trolley, as well as all the plates in the room that had been used. Nolan came toward her and she asked him if they were mad.

"No. Chris said to tell you she loves you. Myra said you were a hoot, and Beckman wanted to fix us a nice picnic basket to take to the woods but I asked him to wait. He also said he'd take care of the young master. That would be Shane."

"I want to go running with you." He nodded and started to unbutton his shirt. "And as soon as you can manage it, I want to be what you are. A panther. I don't want to be left behind when you go for a run."

"I can do that too." His shirt slid to the floor. "You will have to go now. Go to the trees and run. My cat wants to chase you. And when we find you, we'd very much like for you to be naked. He wants to fuck you with his tongue."

Going to the door to the back yard, she turned to him and watched him take off his pants. When he paused and looked at her, she wanted to ask him if he loved her. But she was actually afraid of his answer. When he told her again to go, she nodded once and left the house. She was nearly to the tree line when she heard him roar. Picking up speed, she ran as if her life depended on it, laughing all the way.

Chapter 10

Nolan knew where she was all the time. He played with her, toyed with her fear and fun. When she would drop a piece of her clothing, a shirt here, her bra there, he would pick them up and take them back to the same spot where his clothing was. When he found her panties, soaking wet with her juices, his cat buried his nose in them before taking them, too, back to the rest of her clothing. When he found the last item, her shoe, he moved through the woods, stalking her. Playtime was over.

You should know I can smell you. How aroused you are, and needy. You're very wet, aren't you? She told him she'd had to stop twice to wipe the juices from her thighs. *That's going to cost you, love. No one messes with my cream unless I say so.*

Her laughter made his breath catch. She really was having fun. And he, more than anything, wanted to assure her that he did indeed love her. Knowing that she had her doubts earlier had prompted him to make sure she not only knew that she was his one and only, but that he did indeed love her with all of his being. Both he and his cat did. Finding her near a tree, he watched her try to hide herself from him when a branch broke nearby. He dropped to his belly and waited for whatever it was to show itself. The herd of deer startled him as much as it did Rylee.

Oh, Nolan, you should see the deer. They're so beautiful. He told her he thought so as well. *You're here? Of course you are. I've never been out of your sight, have I? But I've never been this close to them before. Why is it they're not running from us?*

You have managed to cover the entire woods with your scent, and they don't know that the woods don't always smell of you. They just think it's a natural scent of humans roaming all over now. Also, I'm not moving, so they don't know I'm here as yet. He looked over at her as she watched them. *If you could see you as I do now, you'd be amazed. I don't think I've ever seen you look so lovely before.*

She looked in his direction, but he knew she couldn't see him yet. The woods were dark enough here that his coat blended well with the area around him. *Where are you? And how do I...what is so different about me now than any other time you've seen me naked? I'm just the same.*

No, you're not. You're a natural beauty there standing against the tree. Your hair is a perfect match to the bark behind you, your body is captured in the moons rays, and each part of you is highlighted as if you were a goddess on display. I can see your hard nipples now, and your pussy is glistening in the light. And even though you are standing as still as a stone on the ground, I can see your heart beating in your breasts, your breaths as you breathe lightly so as not to disturb the deer. You are a wonderment to me. Beautiful and strong, and even venerable too.

I love you, Nolan. I...I've never said that to anyone and really meant it. I tell Shane, and I told my sister when she was alive, but I love you differently. With not just my heart, but all of me. He told her he loved her too. *You don't have to say it back to me. I mean, you've said it before, but it's okay if you didn't...I'm fucking this up.*

You're not. You're scared. So am I. She asked him why he'd be scared. *Because you're going to need me sometimes, and you're not used to needing anyone. But let me tell you something you might not already know...I need you just as much, if not more. You're my love. Not my other half, Rylee, but all of me. Without you, I would not live. I wouldn't even want to.*

He stood up and watched her when she moved. The deer scattered, but he only had eyes for her. As she moved toward him, Nolan could only think of one thing, and that was that she was his. And his cat agreed. Moving to her as well, he knew his cat was going to get his fill first, but Nolan was going to take more. He was going to take all of her.

His cat snarled at him when he told him to go easy. But the cat might have been right. She didn't look like she wanted easy. She needed him as much as he did her. When she stopped, his cat moved forward and knocked her to the ground, and when she sat up his cat nudged her back so that she was lying in front of them. Before she could say anything, even if she might have wanted to, his cat was between her legs and licking her cream. Her scream of release echoed around the woods. Birds took flight when she screamed again.

"Please. I need more." The cat understood her and slammed his tongue deep within her. When Rylee screamed, he put his paws on her thighs and held her as he continued eating her...not just eating her, but devouring her. His cat had never been this aggressive with her before, and he might have been nervous but for the many times that Rylee came while he took her. When he lifted his head and looked at her, Nolan only had a moment to wonder what he was going to do when he lunged at her and bit deeply into her thigh. It was the first time that he'd marked her, and apparently he was going to make it good. Her scream this time had Nolan begging to be freed from his cat, who held her like his life depended on it.

I'm sorry, love. She told him it was all right, but Nolan didn't think so. When the cat finally let her go and then Nolan, he moved up her body slowly to see how badly she'd been bitten.

It was an open wound. Her bone was broken, and he could see that he'd bitten her through. Licking the bloodied mess, he kept telling her how sorry he was when she jerked him up by his hair and told him to do it.

"I'm bleeding out." Nolan shook his head but could see that she was right. She was losing blood too fast. Even her heart rate was slowing. "End this. Now, Nolan. I'm not going to die out here naked in the middle of the woods. And if I do, I will haunt you for the rest of your days, I swear it. Do it now."

He really had no choice. Nolan was pissed…his cat had done this, and while he wasn't sure how, he had a feeling that Rylee was in on it too. He let his cat consume him as he lunged at her soft belly and bit her hard enough again to break several ribs. Nolan begged her to forgive him even as she held him to her.

Her screams tore at him. Even as he lay there with her, his cat's mouth holding her, Rylee stroked him. Ran her hand up and down his fur as if they were not fighting a very serious game of life and death. When she finally passed out, he held her just a little longer, loving her and telling her she'd be all right. Then his cat simply let go, and Nolan moved to cradle her into his arms.

"You did good, big boy." Her voice was weak, but he could tell she was far from out of the woods. She'd lost a great deal of blood, and that alone gave him pause to move her just yet. "I love you, Nolan. Very much."

"I love you too." She grinned but didn't open her eyes. His heart twisted in his chest, he was so worried for her. "You owe me for this. I never got to make love to you out here in the woods. I'm sort of disappointed in you, if you want to know the truth."

"Yeah, but you'll get over it soon enough." She coughed slightly, and he held her while she leaned over and threw up twice. "I don't feel so good. I think maybe I've been bitten by something."

Her laughter was low, but he laughed with her. What a time for jokes, he thought, and wiped her mouth off with his hand. Soon, he could hear her heart rate picking back up, and her breathing seemed to be better. Not wanting to leave her but knowing he had to, he moved to get their clothing so he could take her home. As he moved away from her, keeping her in his sights, he reached for his brother Micah to tell him what he'd just done.

Good, I'm glad to hear that. I was going to suggest it, but you've been...anyway, I'm thrilled to know that it's done. But there are a few things you need to be made aware of. David Cole is gone. I had two men on him, but he got away from them. Well, he killed one and injured the other, so that puts him on my list, as well as Paddy's, as one of the men were his. I don't know if he's stupid enough to come there, but you should be aware of it. Nolan pulled on the pants he'd brought out with him and then pulled on his boots as Micah continued. *And...and you should know if she's not better by day after tomorrow, you're going to have to explain to Mom and Grandma why she can't attend the biggest event of the decade.*

Mother fuck. I forgot. He heard his brother laugh at him. *I'm going to be in so much...do you think it will matter to them that I didn't want to do this, the cat did?*

No. I don't think it will matter one bit. And so you know, I'm going to help you out with this because you're my brother. Nolan asked him how. *I'm not going to tell Reggie so she can protect you. You'll be all on your own.*

You're going to pay for this. Actually, Nolan felt pretty good, all things considered. He had a mate, and she was going to be a cat when she woke up. And he had the best family in the world, bar none. *Micah, I'm in love with her. But I guess you know that. But there is something I've wanted to tell you for a while now, I'm sorry. For everything. I should have...I should have come to you when I saw I was failing. It was wrong of me to treat you all the way I did when I knew...I knew that I couldn't do it on my own.*

You didn't fail, Nolan. Never that. What you did was wonderful, not just for the homeless but for a lot of people that just wouldn't have some of the benefits that they do now because of you. And the fact that you nearly made it happen is the...Dad would be so proud of you. Christ, he would have loved it. Nolan told him what Rylee had done to him the day that he'd taken her to the shelter. *I knew I was going to like her. Man, she's perfect for you. All macho and shit like you are. Do you think she'll have children just like her? I hope so. Can you imagine what kind of hellions you'll have?*

I don't even want to think about it. But he did now as he moved over her body to make sure that nothing was sticking her or crawling on her since he'd been gone. Now all he could think about was her having his child, their child. *Micah, I need a favor. Will you ask Grandma if she still has my ring? The one she gave me when Dad died?*

I'm sure she does. I'll even go you one better. I'll take it to the jewelers myself and have it cleaned for you. He thanked him and nearly closed the connection before Micah spoke again. *Watch your back. I'm not sure what this bastard Cole has in mind, but it can't bode well for you guys.*

When has it ever? Micah agreed and closed the connection between them.

Nolan looked down at Rylee as she rested peacefully. "You're going to have to help me out with Mom and Grandma. Because you made me do this to you, we might not get to go to the charity event they're helping the shelter with."

Dressing her was by far harder than he'd thought it would be. He was more used to undressing her rather than trying to figure out the way things worked in the opposite direction. The bra was the most complicated. How did he get her breasts into the little cup things and make them even? He thought the straps at her shoulder's looked painful, and wondered why she even bothered. Then when he got it on her, he realized they did sort of make them look secure. Not a sexy word, he supposed, but that's what it looked like. Then there were her panties.

Panties. Now there was a sexy fucking word, he told himself. But as far as functional and covering her? Not so much. They covered her for the most part, but that was about it. They rode up her ass cheeks, a place that he really would like to explore some time, and they didn't secure anything. Just thinking of how wet they'd been when he'd found them had him pausing several times to adjust himself. By the time he was finished, he was soaking wet from exertion, as well as hard as a rock.

Picking her up to carry her back to the house, he thought of how much he was going to enjoy watching her run as a panther, and also wondered what sort of colors she'd be. Her hair was light, almost blonde, so he figured she'd not be solid like him, but her eyes, as blue as the sky in summer, were going to stick out as well. Smiling as he entered the house, he looked at Beckman as he stood there.

"She made me." He grinned at him and nodded. "Do you think perhaps you can make me something to eat and bring it to me? I want to get her into the shower...I think I want to try to get her a little cleaned up, but I'm starving too."

"Yes, my lord." The man had been calling him that for days now, and no matter how many times he'd asked him not to, he did it anyway. "Lady Constance called back. I told her that you and the missus had run an errand. I believe she understood. She said she would meet with you and the rest of the people tomorrow afternoon at the mall in the food court. I will say this, she did sound upset with something. I don't believe, however, it was with the mistress. Shall I call her back and reschedule?"

"Not yet." He looked down at the sleeping beauty in his arms. "For all I know she could be up before me tomorrow and out chasing rabbits for the fun of it. We'll just wait and see how she feels tomorrow. All right?"

"Yes, my lord. Lord Micah called as well. He informed me of the man who is Master Shane's father. I have asked to have more magic put around the house and the two of you. Also, Myra has taken precautions for Master Shane." He didn't want to ask what sort of things she'd done for Shane, so only nodded. Going to the door, he turned back when Beckman said his name. "The vampire that was here earlier, he has given young Shane a gift of himself. I don't know if you were aware of it or not, but it will also keep him safe. He will...harm will not come to him as it would have before, and I think they have a connection not unlike the one that the vampire has with your mate."

"Good. I think. Do you...should he have asked for permission before doing that?" Beckman said that he didn't believe it was necessary to ask. "All right. I'm going up now. If anyone calls...I don't know. Handle it if you can, or come get me. I'll have her in bed in about twenty minutes, I guess."

"I shall bring you up a tray. And if you ask the house to help you, it will." Beckman turned his back to him and opened the refrigerator. Nolan wasn't sure what that meant, but he nodded and moved to the stairs. This house was really going to be strange getting used to.

Nolan thought when he was standing in the stall with a very naked, wet Rylee in his arms that dressing her had been a piece of cake compared to this. Even doing something as simple as washing her hair had turned into a mess. He'd dropped the bottle on the floor, and before he could figure out how to pick it up without dropping Rylee, he realized most of it had already spilled down the drain. It wasn't long before a mound of bubbles grew large enough to reach his hips. Christ, this was a horrible idea, he thought.

"I could really use some help." The wall shifted next to him, and he watched in fascinated horror as it moved to have two large pieces of tile branch out like arms. Having no idea what he was supposed to do now, the bubbles just disappeared and the bottle he had dropped was filled again and just seemed to levitate to his hand. He sat it gently on the wall shelf as he tried to think what he could do. Then it hit him.

Hanging her arms over the protrusions, he wasn't surprised this time when something came out of the tile again and wrapped around her waist. She was secure now, and he could use both hands to wash her. Thanking the house, he filled his sponge with soap and began scrubbing the twigs and other things he'd not seen when he'd dressed her in the woods. Nolan began talking to keep himself to keep from thinking about what the house had done for him.

"I have to go into the office tomorrow. Caroline James missed her appointment on Monday and I told her I'd help her out by coming in on a Saturday for her. She's going to have twins in a few months. While she's not a cat but a lioness, she's having a hard time of it with her husband gone a lot. He's in the service right now and is expected to come home in a few weeks. Hopefully before his sons are born." He filled the sponge again as he continued. "David is on the run. I'm not really sure what he thinks he's doing right now, but if he comes here, he'll get what he deserves. Micah told me yesterday that his wife left him, and her daddy is taking care of things. I'm not sure I want to know."

"He wants to use me and Shane to bargain for his inheritance back." Nolan was on his knees in front of Rylee when she spoke. "You look very good there. Why don't you...eat me?"

Looking up at her, all he could do was stare at the picture, a very lovely and sexy picture she made standing there with her body draped over the wall. Eat her. That thought, along with a great many others, looped around in his head until he was dizzy with them. When she prompted him again, he smiled.

Dropping the sponge to the tile floor, he pulled her forward and buried his mouth over her nether lips. Christ, she tasted so good, and when he slid his hand up her leg to her opening, she cried out while riding his mouth and fingers as he fucked her this way. When the water was turned off, he looked up at her with his tongue worrying her clit that was peeking so sweetly from her pussy. He'd thought she was gorgeous before, but right now, she was simply the most beautiful creature he'd ever seen.

She rode his mouth as he drank from her. Every time she came, her body would flood his mouth with her juices. Her scent, the cat was there now and was making his wild to take her, but Nolan was going to have his fill first, and to hell with the cats for now. When he stood up and pulled her from the wall, it moved back the way it had been, a smooth surface that he pressed her against as he took her mouth. Lifting his head from hers, just enough to whisper to her, he could see the desire in her eyes was as high as his was.

"I'm going to fuck you here." Her moan was enough to have his balls tighten to him. Lifting her up by her ass, he filled her quickly and fucked her in long hard strokes as he continued to watch her face. "You're so beautiful. The way your eyes widen when I touch that spot in you that is all mine."

"Make me come." He told her she was too greedy. "I am. Make me come please. I need to feel you come inside of me and bite me when you do. I want to mark you. Sink my teeth into you. My cat, I can feel her there too. She wants you, to taste you as you did me."

He needed it. Needed to feel her bite him, mark him as hers. As he fucked her harder, no longer needing to hold back, he felt his teeth shift in his mouth and knew that this bite was going to be different, the mark would be permanent. As she screamed out her release, her body hard beneath his, he bit her, tore into her neck like he was taking her life. And when she did the same to his shoulder, breaking not just flesh but his bones as well, he too cried out as his mouth filled with her hot-spiked blood. Nothing could have prepared him for the immediate and profound connection that snapped into place.

Her nails dug into his back as his cock filled and stretched again. Even as he continued to move in and out of her, she held him to her, her body humming beneath his hands as he held her to him. When she roared out, her cat running along her skin as she came again, his own moved too, seemingly chasing hers as they moved over their bodies. This time when he came, filling her almost violently, he threw back his head and cried out. He wanted the world to know that Rylee was his now and forever.

Holding her up was tricky. He wanted to lie down and take a nap, but she was limp in his arms again and he didn't want to drop her. Lifting his head from her shoulder, licking the last of her blood from the now scarred mark, he smiled when she did.

"You're supposed to be out for at least a couple of days when you're converted, did you know that? Not that it matters, I guess, but I should know that you're never going to conform to things like rules and norms. But now we'll have to get all dressed up and go to the charity event at the shelter in a couple of days." She told him she was sorry. "I don't think you are, actually. Like me converting you, I think you planned this all along. I'm going to have to keep my eye on you a little better, I think."

"I think your eyes are on me enough." She stretched, and his body reacted to having hers slide over his. "You're so hard. Not just that wonderfully talented cock of yours, but all of you."

Her hands moved over his body and gave him strength. Lifting her up, he moved them out of the stall to the sink, where he sat her down. Handing her a thick, warm towel, he dried himself as he kept an eye on her. She really had recovered very quickly, and he was sure there was going to be a relapse or something. He wanted to be there to catch her should she fall. But then nothing she would ever do, he thought, should surprise him.

"I don't have anything to wear to this thing. From what I've heard, it's dressy." He told her it was. "Shane either. I mean, he can go, right? Do we have time to go shopping for something nice?"

"Yes. We'll make the time. And I want him there. My family is going too. And he's my family, so yes, he can go." He wrapped the towel around his waist when someone knocked on the door. "That would be my dinner. I had no idea at the time I asked for it you'd be up to take part of it."

"I'm starved too." When she stood up, he watched her carefully. "I really do feel pretty good. Fantastic, actually. Now go and get our food, and maybe you should tell him to bring more while you're at it."

Nolan was smiling when he opened the door. Beckman was there, but he wasn't alone. The woman behind him, with an equally large tray, moved into the room and set up the table that Nolan had never noticed before. As they began laying out what looked like a feast at Thanksgiving, he thought that perhaps this was going to be too much, and smiled when Rylee came out of the bathroom wrapped up in a snowy robe. Another thing he'd never seen before.

"My lady and lord, I have taken the liberty of bringing up a larger portion of food than you requested. There is also a pitcher of juice here you both should drink down. As always, it will refill until you are finished." He wondered briefly if the food would as well when Beckman turned to Rylee. "A seamstress has been called, my lady. She will arrive in the morning to help you with your dress. Also, a stylist will be on hand to help you with your hair and anything else you might need. Master Shane will be fitted as well, but his tux will be brought here to do so while your dress will need to be made first. I do hope you find this satisfactory?"

"I do." Rylee picked up a slice of toast and three pieces of bacon as she continued. "I don't do heels. I have a bad knee, and I'll be in pain if I have to wear them for very long. Like four minutes tops."

"Not any longer, my lady." With that, Beckman and the woman left them, and Rylee sat on the chair nearest the table. Nolan sat across from her. Then she asked him what Beckman had meant.

"You're a panther now. Any injuries or scars you had before are gone. Tats too, though I've never seen one on you. Not only would you be able to wear heels, sexy ones I'm hoping, you'll not hurt at the end of the night either. You'll heal a great deal faster as well." He went to the bathroom again and pulled the matching robe to hers from behind the door, just knowing it was going to be there. As he sat down, he watched her fill her plate like she'd not eaten in years. Laughing, he did the same. "You'll need to eat more meat now. Red, but not necessarily bloody. Also, we have to drink more juice. In talking to my brother Joey, he said that magic drains us pretty quickly, and juice, natural juice, helps to combat any kind of after affects we might have."

"All this is very strange; you know that, right?" He nodded as he dug into the fluffiest eggs he'd ever eaten and moaned. "Yeah, you should try this. All these things in this cheesy sauce are so good. I don't know what he calls it, but that man is a keeper. But if he cooks like this all the time, I'm going to be as big as a house and then some."

The breakfast casserole was indeed good. The potatoes and cheese along with the eggs were done just right, as were the onions and peppers that had been baked right into it. The ham was in thick yet bite-sized chunks, and the bacon that had been sprinkled on the top was still crisp as well. As he took a second helping of everything, Rylee handed him a homemade biscuit with butter and honey on it as she ate the last two slices of fried ham.

"You won't, by the way." She asked him what he meant. "Get fat. You might put on a few pounds as you get older, like Grandma and Grandda have, but you'll never be fat. We have a higher metabolism, as well as a higher overall body temp. Besides that, you're too energetic, and cats rarely get fat simply because we're a great deal more active than humans are."

"Good to know." As she lay back on the chair, he could see the lines of exhaustion around her eyes. "I wonder if I'll ever feel this good again. I feel like I could take on the world and win. I mean, I will admit that I'm tired right now, but it's not like a stressful tired. More like...well, that I'm exhausted from working hard."

He thought about telling her he thought David might show up there, but she was happy and he didn't want to spoil it. Besides, he had a feeling that if the man showed up now to take her on, he was going to be in for a very rude awakening. And Nolan was going to enjoy watching him go down. When he noticed she'd fallen asleep, he picked her up and put her back in the bed. When she rolled to her side, he noticed she was naked now and wondered if the robe was back in the bath room. Taking his in there, he saw that not only was the one she had on there, but it was dry as well. By the time he was ready to crawl in the bed with her, the room was back to its pristine state and all the dishes, as well as the table and chairs, were gone. Nolan thought perhaps he could get used to this.

Chapter 11

David sat on the hotel bed and thought about his day so far. Four days ago he'd been summoned to his grandmother's home to have his life ruined. Why the hell, after all this time, someone had decided to get a burr up their ass about him was beyond him. Motherfuckers.

The kid was first and foremost his biggest issue. Fourteen some odd years, and that little bit of shit was coming back to bite him in the ass big time. Had Shelby just shut up and signed off on the papers he'd told her to, everything would have been rosy for him. He might not have sold the house out from under her...but then on second thought, he would still have done it. He wouldn't have paid her as he'd promised—that much was a given— but he might have been less pursuant in making her pay for every little thing he could gouge her for. Then there was the fact that all this had come around just when he was having himself a nice little thing with the woman that lived across the street from his current home. Becky's home, he supposed now. The timing could not have been worse.

The money from selling the house when he had was what he was living off right now. Had he not had the foresight to do that, he'd be living in a cardboard box. He had put the money in a safety deposit box and had kept adding to it whenever he was in the bank. Mostly it was Becky's money. He'd buy something and take it back later just to have the cash, since Becky had started to question his every move and purchase. But as far as he was concerned, her money was his anyway. David wished now that he'd left her when he'd figured out that she was boring. He could have been getting some settlement money right now, and that would have been handy in taking care of this business with his first wife. Christ, now this.

He looked over at the paper that had been left on his doorstep that morning. The hotel had asked him if he wanted it delivered, and like a fool he'd said sure. Now there his picture was, blazing across the front of it like a beacon on a lighthouse. And the headline under it had made him slightly ill.

"Dead Beat Dad, David Cole Kicked Out of His Life." His life, as he'd read about it, was much better on paper than it had been in real life. At least it was to him. He had even highlighted the things he found to be untrue, and wanted to talk to his attorney about them. There was no reason for them to print shit about him that wasn't true. It was bad enough that the stuff that was true was there. He glanced at the time on the television and thought about his lawyer. Whenever the little bastard called him back, David was going to get a retraction as well as a public apology from the fucking papers. Picking up the paper, he looked at the items that had been listed.

Limo driver and car. Wrong. He had them, he supposed, but he rarely used them. For one thing, he was pretty sure that Poser, his father-in-law and the meanest man in the world, had paid the guy to keep tabs on his every move. It was easier for him and a good deal more private to drive himself where he wanted to go. It was hard sometimes, finding the right parking spot as opposed to just being dropped off, but he didn't like the constant questions about where he was and how long he was going to be gone. And he could also stay out as late as he wanted under the guise of being at work. Smiling, David thought of how easy that one was to use. But in reality, David hadn't worked in twenty years.

Credit cards with a seemingly endless supply of money. Also not true. He couldn't spend over five hundred dollars in one place unless he called his wife. Becky had cramped his style a great many times when he'd wanted to have some fun. Twice he'd been told yes on something, and the rest? He'd been denied. Why the hell couldn't he just buy what he wanted when he wanted? It wasn't as if she didn't have the money. And when good old Dad passed, she'd have his too. Why did she feel she had to have her hand in all his goings on?

There was mention of the private jet, as well as the yacht. He'd been on both and wasn't impressed. The jet couldn't be just taken wherever he wanted to go without a formal written itinerary, and the boat was only big enough for a smallish party of about two hundred people. Not to mention when he'd taken it out alone, the staff wouldn't let him have his fun. No fucking of the guests, and when asked, the crew told him they were off limits too. Why were they paying these people if they had all these things that they wanted and not him?

Parties. Okay, there were endless parties, but most, if not all of them, were without his family. He supposed if he'd been there when his first daughter had been born, Becky might have let up on that a little. But when he'd missed the second daughter coming into the world, she'd threatened him with no more sex or children. Not really much of loss there as far as he was concerned. He could and did get it as much as he wanted from whoever he wanted. A week after the second brat had come into the world, screaming and shitting everywhere, he'd gone in and had his own little procedure, and taken care of that issue right away.

Kids were useless as far as he was concerned. And they were messy and loud. When he was home, which lately hadn't been often, he had no desire to help with homework, see what they'd done for the day, and he most certainly didn't want to have anything to do with teacher's conferences. Teachers, as far as he was concerned, were only teachers because they were too stupid to do anything productive.

David laid the paper in front of him to see what else he'd marked. When he read down the list, he realized he'd missed something. Vacations with his family and how he'd missed all of them. Big. Fucking. Deal. He'd missed them simply because he didn't want to be stuck in some hotel on an island with nine thousand other people only to hear his family bitch about how he wasn't spending time with them. Nope, not going to happen. The point of missing the vacations with his family was that he didn't like his family. They were a way to what he wanted and nothing more.

When the phone rang, he moved to pick it up, holding the paper so he could go over things with his attorney now that he'd gotten up off his ass and called him back. But before he could launch into his list of bitches, the woman at the other end started talking. He had to ask her twice to slow down and repeat herself before David sat on the bed to listen carefully.

"As I have said, you are no longer being represented by this firm. There would be a conflict of interest in another matter, and going to court with you would not be welcome by all parties." David asked her what she was talking about. "Your grandmother, sir. She is suing you as well. And representing you in the matter of the divorce of you and your wife would not work, because we have a prior commitment to her and her family."

"But I am her family. She's my grandmother, you moron." The woman said nothing, and David started again. "Listen. This is just stupid. Let me talk to Conrad Morgan. He'll be able to tell you what's what. My family is the Cole's, in the event you missed that bit of information when you were no doubt fucking around. Get him on the line."

"Hold please." He could hear the tightness in her voice but really didn't care. When she came back and told him he was being transferred, David felt empowered again, like things were finally looking up. But the woman at the other end of the phone when it was picked up was not who he wanted to talk to. Not now and not ever if he could manage it.

"David, I don't have time for your bullshit. Leave my attorneys alone and get up off your lazy ass and get your own. I hear there are any number of free ones you might be able to afford." He sat down on the bed when his grandmother laughed. "Or do you expect me to get one for you? If you do, I'm afraid you're out of luck. I have neither the time nor the inclination to help you anymore. Not after what I've found out about you and your treatment of your children."

"Why not? I never wanted them in the first place, so why are you punishing me with them?" She laughed again, and he wanted to go to her house and hit her. "You can't do this to me, Grandmother. I'm your only heir. That kid? He won't know what to do with all your money. Besides, I have plans for it. I want to use it the way you should have been doing all these years."

"Had I used the money the way you would have, I'm afraid there wouldn't be any for you in the first place. You would have had me as broke as you are now if I had done just half of the crap you tried to pull. Do you honestly think that everything needs to be handed to you on a silver...no...make that a golden platter? David, you're going to have to make do with what you have now. Just think of this as a learning experience for you. You might find that you like being poor." He told her that he didn't think so. "Be that as it may, you are. And when Phil Poser gets finished with you, you're going to be more than broke. And what I have in store for you will just put you over the edge, I'm afraid."

He was more afraid of Poser than he was of his grandmother if the truth were told. He knew that he'd had her wrapped around his finger before and would so again soon, but Poser was a man that got what he wanted at any cost. Murder was not something he would shy away from. With his grandmother, he would just have to wait her out, or have her killed. But Poser...well, he hated having him pissed off at him.

"You're doing this because of that kid and his mother, aren't you? She didn't mean anything to me. And him even less. Christ, do you expect me to start acting like he's my son now? After all this time? I don't even want the ones that call me 'daddy,' much less one I've only seen once in his entire life." She didn't say anything. "Look, to make you happy, I'll try to work on being someone you want me to be when I'm around you. He'll be the best son in the world when we come to visit, but that's it. I'm not going to support him. I'm not going to take him to little league games. And I will never have him come around for a daddy visit unless it's to see you. Will that make you stop this ridiculous campaign to make me out to be some horrible person?"

"You are a horrible person, David. But until this very moment, I never knew just how horrible you really are. My God, that is your flesh and blood. Don't you even care what happens to him?" He started to answer, but she cut him off. "I'm finished with you. As of this very moment, I'm done. Don't call this house again or I'll have you arrested for harassment. And you are certainly not to bother me again, even if you see me out in public. As of now, you are dead to me."

The line went dead, and David sat there listening to the tone for a full minute before it occurred to him when she called him back to apologize she'd not be able to do that with the phone off the cradle. After replacing the handset, he moved to sit at the little desk that had come with the room to wait her out. Soon she'd realize her mistake and call him back, telling him what a fool she'd been. Any time now. He shifted on the uncomfortable chair and wanted to complain again about the accommodations.

No matter how hard he'd argued with the manager, no one would go out and get him a better desk to use, along with a state of the art computer. He had the money for it, but they only laughed at him. Apparently they didn't do that sort of thing for just guests. He supposed if he owned the hotel, as he was pretty sure his grandmother did, he'd have a gold plated everything, and even a hooker in his bed should he need one.

It was nearing midnight when he realized she might not be calling him back. Then around one in the morning he'd realized something else. He was alone in this world. No one loved him. It took him nearly two hours to console himself enough to go to sleep, and that was fitful. Why, he kept asking himself, why was he the bad guy?

Upon waking the next afternoon, he felt better. Not as rested as he should have been given how much they were charging him for this room, but after he finished up with the things he wanted to do today, things would be back to normal. Well, as normal as he could make them without having a wife and her money.

The first thing he was going to do was go and make amends with his son. Or at least the appearance of making amends. And if that didn't pan out, he'd just make him obey. He was his father, after all. His grandmother would take that as a good sign and not take him out of the will if the kid would just meet him halfway. Then when that was set and his grandmother was no longer a problem but worm food, he'd toss the kid away like the old rags that he was, as far as David was concerned. Calling a limo service, he looked up the address of Nolan Bentley and took a shower. Things were about to be in his favor.

But as soon as he pulled into the long drive, he knew he was at the wrong address. This place was a horse farm, not the home of a doctor. When he was about to tell the driver what an idiot he'd been, the boy walked out of the barn and stared at him. Maybe this man, this Nolan person, was a vet and he'd gotten it wrong. Not that he cared. But David got out of the car just as the kids leaned back against the fence.

~~~

Shane knew who it was. What he wasn't sure of was why he was there. His aunt had dropped him off here an hour ago and he was learning the ropes. Walter had been showing him around until about ten minutes ago when he just needed a break. Walter, as it turned out, was becoming a good friend to him, and a sort of big brother too.

Shane liked the big barn and all, but the horses were scary. Not all of them. There were a couple that he could touch, but for the most part, they were skittish, Walter had told him, more afraid of him than he was of them. Shane supposed that was true, but he didn't care for anyone or anything not trusting him. When Mr. Cole got out of the car and the driver pulled over to the barn, Shane watched his father closely.

"I've come here to see if we can get along. My grandmother, your great grandmother, has it in her head that you're the cause of my being a pain in her ass right now. So you'll come along with me, and we'll pretend we're good friends now." Shane didn't say anything but backed up to almost over the fence when he stepped too close. "You'll listen to me, boy, or so help me I'll...I'll take away your phone."

"I don't have a phone. And even if I did, you wouldn't get it. And I don't want you as my friend any more than I want you as my father." He looked confused. "What are you doing here? My aunt and Nolan are working, but there is an entire staff around if you try to hurt me."

"I don't want to hurt you, not yet at any rate. I don't want you at all, but I won't hurt you if you do what I tell you. If you refuse to cooperate, there will be hell to pay. I need you to like me right now. My grandmother has taken me out of her will, I think, and if you and I are together and act like we like one another, perhaps she'll change her mind. I need that money. You don't. Just do as I say and I'll give you...I'll pay you to come along with me. Ten bucks. How about that?" Shane said nothing, but wondered what the heck the man was talking about. "Come on, we'll go over to her house right now and show her we love each other."

"I don't love you. I don't even like you. You aren't anything at all to me." Shane saw Walter come out of the barn and stand next to him, but didn't say anything. "You should just get back in your fancy car and leave me alone. I don't want anything to do with you. And if Nolan or the others knew you were here, I think they'd be pretty mad at you too. Just go away and leave me alone."

"Don't you think that's what I want? Christ, kid, I'd just as soon you were out of my life completely, but here you stand as a monument to the worst mistake I ever made." That hurt, but not as much as his next words did. "Getting caught trying to get your stupid mother to do what she should have done without any problems was really dumb, don't you think? And your mom? Why the hell did she not just do what she was told? My life would be so much better if she had just listened. But I didn't kill her, like that aunt of yours is saying. I was—"

"I think it's time you left." Walter had moved closer to him and stood up to Mr. Cole when he told him to go away. Shane knew that look from Walter. It was one that you never wanted to see directed at you. "This is my little brother, you fucking piece of shit, and if you come any closer to him, I'm going to use all my skills as a bully and mess you up. He's asked you to go away, and I think that's really good advice."

Shane wondered if his aunt was paying Walter to say those things, and realized that she'd not do that. Whatever Walter was saying, he was saying it because he wanted to. That alone gave Shane more confidence in what was going on. He looked at Mr. Cole again.

There was something very unstable about him, and Shane didn't want anyone to get hurt by him. Didn't want either him or Walter to get hurt, as a matter of fact. When Mr. Cole told Walter again to get on back in the barn where he belonged, Walter finally looked at Shane.

"Go in the house." Shane shook his head at Walter and told him he wasn't leaving him to be hurt. "Go in and call the police, and then call your aunt. This man is nuts. And when he comes at us, 'cause he will, I'd rather you didn't get yourself hurt by flying fists. Mine in particular."

"You won't hurt me on purpose. But I'm not leaving you out here to deal with him on your own. He'll hurt you. He's like what you were telling me your dad was. An ignorant bastard that hurts because he can." Walter stared at him for several seconds before he nodded and looked at Cole again.

That was when Shane noticed that some of the hands he'd met earlier today were now standing near him and Walter. The big man, Mr. Ted, had a whip in his hand, and Shane noticed that another man had a shovel. He was leaning on it, but Shane had a feeling that he could use it like a good weapon if it came to that. Miss May, the cook from the big house, was standing on the steps with a phone at her ear. Allen Black, a man that he'd met a few days ago, was leaning against the big limo. They were looking like they were relaxed, but he would bet all the money he had in his pocket, all forty-six dollars, that they'd attack if needed. Mr. Cole was a dead man if he tried anything. He looked around too, as if just noticing that they were no longer alone.

"What the hell have you done, kid? This was just going to be me and you. These people are going to make it hard for me to get you to come with me, don't you think? I just wanted to take you to my grandmother's, but now you've gone and made me mad. I'm not a nice person when I'm all riled up, so you know." Shane told Cole that it didn't matter to him if there were nine thousand people there telling him to go with him, he wouldn't anyway. "But you don't understand what you're costing me. Or you just don't care. Your mother was like that. So long as she had the little things in life, she was just fine. Well, I wasn't. Not with her and certainly not with you. My life is on the shitter because you were born. The least you can do is help me get it back together. Then you can go on hating me for all I care."

Something that his aunt had told him a few months ago came to him then. She told him that hating wasn't worth the energy that it used up in your body. What was worth it was revenge. Then she'd tickled him.

"Mr. Cole, I've told you that I'm not going with you. Now I'd very much like for you to get out of here and never come back. I've got my own family now. And soon they're going to adopt me, so I don't even have to have your last name. So I've no need of you in my life."

Cole's face changed then. He went from being angry to...Shane thought he looked insane. Or in this case, more insane. When he came at him, Mr. Cole did, running like he was a linebacker in a big game, Shane braced himself for the pain. A thought popped in his head in that moment.

The big vampire that he'd met several nights ago was suddenly just there. He had no idea why he'd thought of him, but when he did, he knew...just knew that the man could feel his fear. And when nothing happened, he opened his eyes and looked around. Cole was no longer there. Not even...he wasn't anywhere where Shane could see him. He looked around at the rest of the people there to see who had attacked the man before he could hurt him.

Walter was sitting on the ground, his nose bleeding. Miss May was walking toward them with a large towel in her hand, but she looked calm enough. Mr. Black was talking to the limo driver, and the rest of the men were moving back to where they had been. Shane sat down next to Walter and watched as Miss May helped him with his bloodied nose.

"What happened?" Walter looked at him, then at Miss May as the towel was held to his face. "Did you...I don't know, fall? And where is Mr. Cole?"

"You took care of him."

Miss May said that Walter was to bring her the towel when he was finished with it, and kissed him on the head when she left. Shane was more confused now than before.

"You have some very powerful friends." Shane supposed so. Micah had a lot of money, and Chris and Joey seemed to be made of it. His own aunt had some all the time now that she was with Nolan. But powerful? He didn't understand. "I don't think that guy Cole will be bugging you to go with him again. He's just...wow, he's gone."

"Where?" Shane hated feeling stupid, but right now he did. And clueless. Asking Walter what he meant by "gone" made the man laugh. "This isn't funny. He might come back and get us."

"I don't think so." Before Shane could ask Walter what he meant by that, a car pulled in the drive, spitting rocks and dust everywhere. Aunt Rylee was running toward him even before the engine was off. Then Nolan was coming.

The hug felt like she was trying to squeeze him in half. And he thought a hug had never felt better in his life. Before he could catch his breath when she let him go to hug Walter, Nolan had him in his arms. Shane had never been hugged by a man before coming to this family. Now, Grandda or Grandma would hug him daily. Aunt Rylee did all the time, but this hug, this one from Nolan, felt special. And he knew he'd never have another one from him that would compare to this one. It was a hug of love and support.

"You all right?" He nodded, and Nolan looked over at Walter and asked him the same. "You boys, you...it was scary not to be here, but I guess you handled it all right."

"I don't know what happened to him." Nolan asked him who. "Mr. Cole. He was here one minute and running toward us like he was going to hurt one of us. Then...then he was gone."

"Shane?" He heard his name and they all turned to the barn. There wasn't anyone standing there, and he felt himself moving closer to Nolan. "I can't come out there again, I'm afraid. Once was about all I can handle in one day."

The laughter was forced, even he could tell that, but the voice, he didn't know it. It wasn't until the man came out of the shadows that he realized who it was. Moving slowly to Barron, he could see that he was hurting a great deal.

The closer he got to him, the more he could see. His face was blistered, with pus dripping from some of the open wounds. His eye was swollen shut, his mouth looked lopsided, and his right ear...it looked like it was gone.

"Don't be afraid of me, please. I don't know what I'd do if you were. But know that all of this, this damage to me, was worth it to see you unharmed." Shane assured him that he wasn't hurt, but also told him that he wasn't afraid of him, just concerned. "Good, good. I like you very much, and I could not just ignore your calling to me. This will all heal, I promise you."

"I called to you?" The man nodded, and Shane could see that the burns on his face were also covering his hands and arms. "You don't look so good. Is there anything I can do to help you?"

"You are such a sweet boy. But no. I need more than you can give me. But I would not take from you even if I needed it more than life. To do so would be...the connection between us would be greater than you can imagine." He looked to Shane's right and smiled. "Hello, my dear. You have a wonderful young man here. I do hope you know that."

"I do. Let me help you, Barron. You know that I can now." He shook his head at Aunt Rylee. "Please. You're very hurt. And from what I have gathered, you saved them both by doing what you've done. I can't...you saved my sons for me."

"I would do it all over again for them, and I shall be well soon. But due to this unfortunate incident, I will need to ask you to put off my helping my grandson. I do not have it in me, I'm afraid, to do so now." Nolan moved closer to Barron and let out a low growl. "Young man, if you wish to harm me, you will not have much of a fight, I'm afraid."

"What did you do to him?" Barron took a step back from Nolan, and Shane felt his fear. He wasn't sure how he felt it, but he did as surely as he was standing there. Nolan wasn't threatening him, but Barron was afraid all the same. "Will he come back?"

"Nay. He will never come back, not in any lifetime. He intended to harm them, kill them both, and I'm afraid I let my fury at him do things that are better left unsaid. Both your sons would have been killed should he have ever touched him." Nolan looked at him and Walter and then back at Barron, thanking him. "No need for that, my good man. I have grown fond of the young men here. And since we have a connection, slight as it is, when he was afraid and thought of me, it was the only thing I could do. You need only to know that David Cole is no more."

Shane knew in that moment that his biological father was dead. And for the life of him, he couldn't generate any kind of sorrow. When his Aunt Chris walked by him, he thought for sure she was going to hurt Barron, and Shane moved to protect him by standing in front of him. He had no idea what he could do to save a vampire from a witch, but he'd try. But she stopped him with a smile.

"I won't harm your friend. I'm going to help him should you allow me to do so. I can, like no other, give him what he needs to survive this. Because, contrary to his words, he is in worse shape than he says. And he knows it." She turned back to Barron. "You will take what I offer freely or, so help me, I *will* hurt you, Barron."

"I cannot. To do so would be…you know what it would mean between us." She nodded, and Shane moved closer, trying to figure out what was going on. "Your mate, he will be connected to me as well."

"We're aware of what this means, Barron. But you saved my nephews today, and for that we owe you. For what you did for this family, I would give you more should you only let me." Barron looked at him as he pushed to stand beside him. "Do you think that Shane would want you to suffer? Or Walter for that matter? You saved them at a great cost to yourself. We're all indebted to you."

"She's offering you her blood?" Barron nodded, and Shane was worried for him. He was looking really bad. "Take it. What if...I don't know, what if I need you again and you can't come help me? That would really suck, because I like you and this new life. If I'm killed then...sheesh, Mr. Barron, if it will make you better, then please take it."

"You drive a hard bargain, my young friend." Shane watched him take his aunt's arm. His hands, fingers, too, were peeling away, and he looked like he might lose one of them. When he took her wrist to his mouth, Shane watched. It wasn't sickening, nor did it seem to be painful to Chris, so he moved closer to her to lend her support. This was a fantastic family, he thought. And was glad every day that they'd come into their lives.

Chapter 12

Alta wasn't sure what to think now. She'd never cared for David, but he was her grandson. Kason said her name, so she looked in his direction and nodded that she was all right. She wasn't, she was sure, but for now...she was at peace.

"They found his body about an hour ago. He'd been hit by a car, they believe. What do you suppose he was doing walking along that part of the road at night?" Alta had no idea, but she did have a feeling that the Bentleys had had something to do with it. She wasn't sure what it could have been with him being hit by a car, but she'd bet anything they had. And that didn't bother her either.

"I would say that he was on his way to see his son. Perhaps to...or maybe not...cause him some harm. I think he might have been on the edge when I talked to him earlier. He would have...he would have killed him, I think." The more she thought about it, she knew that was what had happened. Alta looked at Kason. "Do you suppose he meant to kill that young boy? Just for the money? To perhaps be the only one I had left, so I'd leave it all to him?"

"As much as I hate to say it, it was my first thought as well. Money meant a great deal more to him than family, sadly." She nodded, hurt now that the words had actually been said aloud, and sipped her tea. "I think we need something stronger, don't you? I can get us both a sherry. Should you like one?"

"I would love one, but young Shane is coming soon. We're sitting him tonight, remember?" He told her he'd forgotten that. "I'm hoping this will be the first of many such visits. And he has also expressed a desire to get to know his half-sisters. I'm not sure how that will go over, but we're going to try to arrange it."

"He's a good boy. When he called here just this morning, he was very polite and asked after me. I don't think I've had anyone but you ask about my day in many a year." He smiled. "I think we should have a treat tonight. What do you think of ordering a pizza? I'm to understand from his aunt that it is one of his favorite foods."

"I like that idea. And something special for dessert as well. How about...where did I see that? Making your own sundaes. We have time to get things, don't we?" She was warming to the idea. There were funeral plans to make, of course. Rebecca and her family had washed their hands of David the day they'd walked in on him. So it was left to her to make the arrangements. But for now, she was going to enjoy Shane and his youthfulness.

On the computer, she and Kason made a list of things that were needed to make the treat. They even decided to have a make your own pizza too. There really wasn't much to it, and it was going to be far more expensive than simply having one brought to them, but she was going to enjoy it and was sure that Shane would as well. Who knew there were so many things that could be put on a layer of dough and then baked? She thought she might enjoy the one with ham slices and pineapple the best.

"I've talked to my lawyer." Kason said nothing as they sat at her desk. He was on the same side as her as they wrote out their lists. "He has made the necessary changes to my will for things to work out. I'm not...I guess we'll have to change things again now that David is gone, but nothing will change for the young man. He is...he is my heir in all things. I'll leave a bit to the other two, but for the majority of the money and properties, Shane will be a very wealthy young man someday."

"You have plenty of time to make the necessary changes concerning David." She smiled at him. They both knew that she didn't. Not that she was ill, but she wasn't young either. "Would you like for me to call him for an appointment tomorrow after your visit with Nolan and Rylee?"

"They're not going to be happy with me either, I'm afraid. And in truth, I'm looking forward to a good fight with her. She does not pull back in respect to my age or money, and I find that refreshing." He laughed with her. Alta thought of something she'd been thinking about for days now. "Do you suppose when I meet my Maker, He'll wonder why I didn't do something sooner? Try harder to find out if Shane really was his or not?"

"I believe He will think you a good woman who did the best she could with what she had to work with. Why should you have not believed David? He was a good liar and had had a great deal of practice at it. I'm not blaming Shelby in this, but she might have called to ask for help too.

Not that I think she would have—I'm sure stubbornness runs deeply in their family—but it might have helped them." Alta had thought of that too. But she still was riddled with guilt. "You will help the boy and in the end, I'm sure that was what his mother would have wanted all along anyway. For her son to have it better than she did."

And she was going to make sure that he had more. Much more. After talking with Micah and his lovely wife, and then Joseph again, she knew the boy was going to have all that he'd ever need in life with them as his family. Micah had even told her that should she want to do something for him, that the mother was still without a marker to her burial place, and there was a little matter of the house. The one that he'd lived in until David had taken it from them.

"You think he'd want the house for his own?" Micah told her that Shelby had not been ill there, and it would hold his best memories of her. "I think you might be right. I'll make the arrangements as soon as possible. You are a sly one, aren't you, Micah Bentley?"

"I am. Though my wife tends to forget that." Reggie smacked her husband on the arm and reached for one of the tiny bundles that had come with them. Alta had been surprised by that, the children coming to a meeting, but Reggie had told her that she missed them when she left them with their grandmother and needed to have them around. When Reggie stood up and handed her the little girl, Alta fell instantly in love.

"It has been so long since I've held a baby." Reggie told her it was something to get used to, but she was sure it was a thing you never forgot. "Oh, I would imagine. I'm to understand that you're going to adopt more too. That's wonderful of you to take them in."

"They give me hope. I need it more and more, I find. The children will not be of our body, of course, but they'll all own our hearts. I don't think I thought of that when we thought to adopt them." Reggie picked up the other little girl from the seat when she fussed. "When Rylee and Nolan have children, Shane said he was going to love them as his mom would have. With all his heart."

He would too. As the hour came for him to come to visit her, she found herself getting nervous. He'd been there before, of course, but not by himself, and not with the intentions of spending the night. When the doorbell sounded, she moved to the hall to greet him, and had to smile when he came in talking to Kason about his ride over.

"I think that driver is the best. He let me play with the window in the car and hang my head out the top. Not for long though. He said I'd eat a bug or two if I did it coming through the country air. Have you ever done that sort of thing?" Kason took Shane's jacket and told him he had not. "Yeah, I didn't think so. Too undignified for you, I'm betting."

"A man like me does not hang his head out of the top of the car like a puppy on his first outing. But I can see the appeal it would have for a young man like yourself." As Kason leaned over to whisper in Shane's ear, she could hear too. "However, if you'd like to have a race down the banister, I'm sure I can show you how undignified I can be."

"You're on." Shane was still grinning when he spotted her. "Howdy, Grandma. Grandda said to tell you that next time we're going fishing he wants you to come along too. I have my own pole now. Did you know that it's important to learn how to bait a hook properly? I didn't. I hope you're okay with that."

"I am indeed." Alta looked at Kason and could see that they felt the same way. They were in love with the young man. He'd gotten into their hearts, and they were both going to enjoy him as much as he'd let them.

~~~

Rylee turned right, then left in the big mirror. She absolutely hated everything about this dress. The woman that had designed it for her said that it was a perfect foil to her skin tone. But all Rylee saw was a green dress that didn't suit anything about her. And the shoes were ugly. Nolan cleared his throat behind her, and she glared at him in the mirror.

"You look…unhappy." He came more in the room, and she turned to look at him. "Oh my. Do you…I'm not sure how to tell you this, love, but that's ugly. What is that thing on the front of it?"

"She said it would enhance my body. I think she's trying to make me look like I dug around in the dumpster of a clothing store and stapled things together so they'd cover my body. This color looks…is this even a color that is real?" He didn't laugh, for which she was grateful. "I can't go. I want to, really I do, but I can't go in this thing. I will shame your entire family. Not to mention if I move too fast, I might knock a few of them on their asses."

"I hate to admit this, but you really can't go out into public in that thing. It's a good thing that Myra came by and brought you something else." That didn't sound any better than this dress did. She'd seen the dresses that Myra wore and the colors of them. "She said you have to trust her."

"I don't know, Nolan. This thing is important to you and your family. I don't think I can pull off the colors that she picks out to wear." He smiled at her and kissed her on the nose. Just as he stood away from her, she noticed that there were others in the room with them now. "Nolan?"

"They're going to help you get ready. I have my tux in the other room so that when I have to leave, which is soon, I can take it with me. So I won't get to see you until you're at the shelter. I have to go in a little earlier with my brothers to help set up the auction items." She looked at the four women, then back at him. "You'll be fine. Walter and Shane also got you something to wear. I'll see you in a few hours."

After he left her, she stared at the women. The oldest looking one stepped forward and walked around her. Rylee wanted to run and hide somewhere...that was how hideous she felt in this dress. The woman then stood in front of her.

"Did you pay for this?" Nodding, Rylee felt tears fill her eyes. "Well, I'm going to make sure you get your money back. That's the ugliest thing I've ever seen. Did she even know what she was designing? It was supposed to be a formal dress, right?"

"She said that she wanted me to shine." The woman said she wasn't going to shine very much in that thing. "Do you think you can make it work for me? I don't want Nolan to be embarrassed with me."

"Oh honey, there is no hope for that thing. I have something for you that I think...good heavens, I cannot believe that she put this together on purpose." Rylee laughed with her. "My name is Mable, and these are my assistants. We'll have you done up in no time. Oh, and that young man of yours, he has something for you to put with your dress when we're done. So I sort of designed your dress around it."

They worked for an hour just measuring her. When they had her dressed in just her robe, a chair was brought in and her toes and nails were done. It was a luxury that she'd never had before, and found that she really did enjoy it. Then when she was set to dry, another woman came and did her hair.

Rylee had never really liked her hair. It was there, so she dealt with it as best she could without putting any kind of effort in it. Pulling it back into a pony tail when it got to be too long worked best, or she'd hack it off if that too became a bother. As the woman massaged her scalp, she felt her mind drifting away.

Nolan had made love to her early this morning in such a way that she thought for sure she'd never recover. After he'd tied her to the bed, not tightly but enough that she knew she shouldn't work too hard at pulling on the silk scarves, he'd stripped down and stood before her. Christ, the man had a body that made her drool.

"I'm going to touch you now. Not everywhere, but in enough places that you're going to be soaking when I'm finished." She'd told him that she was there already. His "just wait" had her body tingling.

His fingers had moved over her body in a slow measured way. First up her legs, then down them. Over her hips to her breasts. By the time he was touching her neck and shoulders, she wasn't sure if she wanted to kill him or beg him to fuck her. But when he slid his fingers into her pussy and told her to ride them, it was all she could do not to scream out her release.

"You're so wet and hot. If I fucked you right now, your pussy would stretch and swell more for me." Begging, she came to find out, only made him move slower. "I want to drink from you. Taste you when you're aroused this much."

He only lapped at her then. His tongue would brush ever so gently over her clit and make it burn with the desire to be suckled. She wanted him inside of her, his mouth over her in the most intimate of ways. But all he did was tease her, bringing her up and over the edge of pleasure that just never seemed like it was enough. Not until he moved over her.

His cock was leaking profusely by the time he rubbed just the crown over her slit. He held himself, his cock so hard and thick with need he could barely contain himself. Then he moved deeper into her, sliding back and forth, in and out of her until she wanted to jerk free and wrap around him. And when he did fill her, burying himself to his root, Rylee released so hard she felt the corners of her vision narrow to a pinpoint.

"Come again." She bowed up at his command, ready and willing, it seemed, to do as he wanted. And when she came again, screaming out loud enough that she was sure that the entire town heard her, he pounded her through three more powerful climaxes before he emptied himself deep. They both had fallen asleep like they were dead. And now she was being massaged again, but in a less personal way.

By the time she was ready to crawl into bed and say fuck it to all of this, she was too relaxed and comfy to move, they were telling her it was time to be fitted. The charity thing was in two hours.

When it was apparent she wasn't going to see herself, either, until they were done, Rylee got excited. The dress was blood red and fit her body like a glove. Other than the fact that she could tell that it was low cut, there was nothing about it she knew. And when they told her she was finished, she held her breath as she waited for the unveiling of the mirrors.

"I'm afraid." Mable nodded, but she could tell she was pleased as well. "Do you think...well, anything would have been an improvement, but do you think that Nolan will like this? I mean...will he be proud of me hanging on his arm?"

"Why don't you turn around and tell me what you think?" She closed her eyes and turned. And when she thought she was in front of the mirrors, she paused just long enough to let out her breath, then opened her eyes. Nothing could have prepared her for the woman who stared back at her.

"Holy shit." The other women laughed as they gathered up their things. "That's really me. I mean...damn, woman, you did an amazing job."

"I had a very good model to work with, I think." Mabel moved up behind her and had her kneel a little. "Now. I'm to understand that young Shane picked this out himself. He said that his mother had one like it, and at some point it was sold for bills. I'm sorry about that. But when he saw this one, he and Walter put their money together and got it for you."

It was a ruby with smaller cut stones around it. Sadly, her sister's ruby had gone to pay the rent one month. There had been enough left over for them to have a pizza. It wasn't much really, but it had gone a long way to making them happy for a time.

The chain around it was delicate and felt beautiful against her skin. She touched her finger to it to try and stem the tears as they gathered in her eyes. When she moved her head to look down at it, she could see that in the mirror there were smaller stones of the same color throughout her hair. Rylee thought she'd never looked prettier.

"Now, if that mate of yours isn't drooling by the time you get your wrap off, I don't know men like I think I do."

Mable touched her cheek and took the tear away with her. "You and that man of yours are well suited. Did you know he told me to spare no expense in making you happy?"

"That dress was hideous." Mable agreed. "I don't know how to thank you for this. I think you went well beyond what was called for in helping me. I feel wonderfully beautiful."

"You are, my dear. Very much so." As the others left the room, Mable had her turn for her one more time. "I'm to take a picture and send it to your nephews. Is that all right? I won't send it to Walter, of course, until you see Nolan, but Shane will enjoy it. No point in spoiling it for him and you."

The other Bentley women arrived a few minutes after Mabel and her crew left. Reggie was bitching about how hungry she was, and Katie was telling her there would be plenty to eat at the shelter when they got there. As soon as she came down the stairs and they saw her, no one moved.

"My goodness, my lady." Beckman stood there with a tray of drinks in his hand and stared. "If you don't mind me saying so, I don't think I've seen you look lovelier."

"Thank you." Gracie asked her to turn for her and she did. The shoes she had on weren't the least bit uncomfortable, and she even showed them those as well. Chris said she was envious of her being able to wear such a color, and Katie told her they were the prettiest group of young women she'd ever seen.

Several pictures were taken. The three of them, Chris, Reggie, and her. Then of her and Grandma Katie. Beckman took several of them all together, and before long it was time to go. As they were helped on with their wraps, Gracie pulled her aside and asked to speak to her.

"I wanted to tell you that I'm very proud of you." She asked her for what. "For Walter and Shane. But Walter came to see me today. Did you know that? Wanted to know if I would mind if he called me 'Grandma' as Shane did. I felt…well, honored, if you want to know the truth. I felt like he was giving me a great gift by asking me that. And when I told him yes, he hugged me like my Micah did when he was alive. Just full of love and happiness."

"He's a good boy…man, I guess. He just needed someone to believe in him." Gracie told her that not all would have done what she did. "Not everyone would do what you've done either. Taking all of us under your wing. Making us feel like we're your daughters, not just in-laws. You're someone I have come to admire and respect. I don't say that to just anyone."

"I love you, Rylee. Very much so. And the rest of you girls as well." Gracie looked away, then back at her. "You've given me something I thought never to have again. Hope. When my husband died…it was everything I could do to get up every day and move. To breathe when I didn't want to and to just get going. The boys helped me. Howie and Katie, they were my only solid foundation after…I didn't want to live. I had no desire to live without him."

"I'm glad you did. They need you." They hugged tightly as they moved toward the door. "I wanted you to know that I need you too. Without you…I know that I would have failed big time. Not just with Shane, but with all of this."

"You would have done well. Do you want to know why I know that?" Rylee nodded. "When I saw you pick that man up by his balls, I knew you'd be the right fit for this family and that nothing would ever bring you down. You impressed me that day. More than I can say."

They were in the limo when her cell phone rang. She smiled at the picture that came up, and was thrilled to hear from Shane. He started telling her about what they were doing, making pizza for themselves.

"Kason even got that salty fish you like. I told him I'd pass, and you know what he did? He just ate one like it was a grape or something. He said they were really good." She laughed when he did. "And later we're having make your own sundaes. This is the best."

"I'm glad you're having a good time. Your grandma was very nice to watch you. And Shane, I love my necklace. Did you get the picture?" He told her he had, and then told her how beautiful she looked. "I'll make sure you get one of Nolan and me together too."

"And the grandmas too. And Grandda. If you can get all of you together, I'd love that more." She told him she would try. "Hey, I've been thinking about what you and Nolan talked to me about. And I want that. I want you to be…nobody will replace my mom, but I'd like to have you and Nolan as my parents. I know that Walter wants that too."

They'd talked to both of them. And even though Walter was an adult, they told him they'd make it legal if he wanted them to, and give him the same things that Shane would have, any help with college as well as money should he need it. His mother had sent word through Joey that she didn't ever want to see him again, and the sooner he was dead, the better she would like it. Victor Simpson was going to be tried next week for the death of his lawyer, and she was blaming it on her son.

"We'll talk tomorrow when I come and get you. You have fun." He told her he would and told her he loved her. "And I love you. With all my heart."

As soon as the limo pulled up in front of the building, she felt her nerves tense up. As each of them was handed out by the man at the door, she could see the sparkle of the people there. When it was her turn, she looked at Katie and told her she felt sick.

"Nonsense. Go out there and show them what a Bentley looks like when they have someone love them." Nodding, she started out but leaned back in and kissed her on the soft cheek. As soon as she was out of the long limo, she saw him.

Nolan had said he was wearing a tux. What he hadn't told her, and probably should have, was that he looked fucking amazing in the thing. Not only did he wear it like he'd been born in it, but he even had a red rose on his lapel that matched her dress perfectly. As he made his way to her, gliding across the walkway like the cat that he was, she felt her own cat stir in response.

"It's a real shame about this lovely dress." She asked him why. "Because I'm going to let my cat tear it from you later, just before he eats you alive."

"Nolan, I'm not going to be able to stand up if you keep talking like that."

Before he could say anything else, his brother Garth came up behind him and patted him on the back. She'd not seen much of Garth, as he was working to get his own home done before the colder weather set in. Even Tony, who was the quiet one of the family, came to stand with them.

Christ, she thought, men like these brothers should be outlawed in all fifty states. They were much too handsome to be let out in the general population, especially on single women. Married ones too, for that matter. As they made their way to the front of the room, she could see how much work had gone into making this shelter look like a very beautiful ballroom for the very rich and very famous.

Chapter 13

Nolan could not take his eyes off her. Rylee was the most beautiful woman in the room as far as he was concerned, and the way she moved around the room made him think she'd been born to this. Not just money, as he'd been, but to the life of being a cat and his mate. He supposed she had been in a way. And she was working the crowd like it was her business. He overheard her telling someone about their antique place, and mentioning a few of the pieces they already had. She was going to be good at that too, with Barron's help.

He thought about the young man, Dennis, who had met them at the mall yesterday. He'd been terrified of meeting them. And the fact that his mother was afraid didn't help matters either. But when she sat with them, him and Rylee, she started talking like she'd had a built-up list of things she wanted to get off her chest. Most of it centered on her father and what she'd done to hurt him.

"I should have known all the facts before...Mom and Dad were never very good together. They loved each other intensely, but neither of them trusted the other. I have the same kind of...volatile relationship with my husband." Dennis snorted at his mom, but said nothing more. She'd looked hurt when she looked at him. "Ansel, he and my son don't get along."

"Your son?" Constance nodded. "I'm sorry, I thought he was your husband's child. I think even Barron thought that."

"No, he's mine. I had...it's not unheard of for our kind to take two lovers when we're mated. When Dennis—my Dennis's—father and I got together, it was what I had hoped for in a relationship with Ansel. But my life with Ansel wasn't like the one with Dennis...not even close. But when Dennis was killed some years later, Ansel said he'd care for us both and we'd never have anything to worry about ever again. He said he'd even protect me from my dad."

"You didn't need protecting from your dad. Surely you know that." She said she did now. "What are your plans, Constance? This meeting with us, it's not what we set up, is it?"

"No. I want to go to my father. I want to...I would like for him to save my son and to...I need my daddy."

There were tears then, and Nolan had called Barron. He had said he'd take her into his home and lair, but the boy, Dennis, would need to be helped first and foremost. And three hours later, under cover of magic and guard, not only was Dennis converted the night before his birthday, but Barron and his daughter had reunited in a way that made them all think they'd never been parted by lies and deceit. Now all they had to do was deal with Ansel. But Myra said she had that part under control. Nolan certainly hoped so, for all their sakes.

Nolan heard the item he wanted to bid on brought to the front. His mom had donated this, and for the life of him he couldn't think why she'd not gotten her one as well. She had done nothing but talk about the donation for a few days now, and he and his brothers were going to get it for her.

The beautiful frame would be filled with any picture that the buyer wanted. The photography place had also donated sixty-five pictures to be taken, as well as a few prints. His mom had mentioned that she'd not had one of her boys, and they were going to make that happen too.

The bidding went up fast. He was glad now he'd asked the rest of them to chip in, and when the thing got up to nearly six figures, he thought perhaps it was also going to be the biggest amount of money brought in all night. There were some pretty amazing gifts. There was the car that had been donated, as well as the maid service for five years, but all of that meant very little when it came to his mom's happiness.

At one point his mom told him to stop, but Grandda told him to go for it. Then when the woman he was bidding against finally sat down, he thought for sure that it was theirs. Then from the back of the room, someone said six million. All of his brothers told him no. It was a nice gift for a great cause, but that was too much for anyone. Whoever the man was, he wanted this thing badly.

When Barron came to stand next to him, he hugged him tightly. Nolan thought the man had never looked happier, and the woman standing next to him, his lovely daughter, had that same look in her eyes. The person who had outbid him, Barron told them, was him. And he presented the frame and certificate to their mom, just as they had wanted to do.

"You have raised some pretty amazing sons, my dear." She told him she had tried but had little to work with. They all laughed. "Be that as it may, I wanted to give you something, and while I know that they wished to present it to you, I wanted you to know that without their help over the last few days, I would have lost it all. Please take this as a token of my appreciation of your being a wonderful mother."

"You paid entirely too much for it, but I do love it." His mom looked around the table at them all and told them she loved them. "I don't know what I would have done without my boys. And now their wives. I have grandchildren that I love and more to come, I hope. But what I have in them...their father would have been so proud of them." She looked away as she wiped at her tears. And Nolan felt his own eyes fill as he thought of his father and the way his life had been cut so short.

The rest of the evening went well after that. Barron joined them then, as did his daughter. There was a great deal of money made too, much more than he'd thought possible. All in all, it was a very successful night. For everyone. But now he wanted his mate.

He found her ten minutes after the last item was sold. She was talking to a group of women that were thinking of organizing another charity event to help raise money for the food pantry. Not on this scale, they were telling Rylee, but something where they could fill the shelves a couple of times a year and have a little left over to buy some gifts for children who would not have a lot. He kissed her on the neck when one of the women noticed him.

"If you ladies don't mind, I'd very much like to borrow my wife." They all smiled knowingly at him as he pulled Rylee to his body. He was going to make her scream as many times as he could tonight. When she looked up at him, all he could think about was how much he loved her. Taking her out to the gardens behind the building, he pressed her against the wall and kissed her.

"Christ, do you have any idea how much I want you right now?" She rolled her hips to his and grinned. "I want you so badly that my balls ache to be emptied. But that dress is going to get messy when I do."

"I'm wet and have no panties on." He nearly fell to his knees. "And now that you're this close, I'm so wet that I can feel it running down my leg. I want to feel you drinking from me."

Nolan did go to his knees then, glad now that he'd taken her to the darkest part of the gardens and nowhere close to the cameras. When he ran his hands up under her dress, he could feel her heat and her juices. She wasn't kidding about it running down her thighs either...he felt her cream as he moved his hand further up her leg.

"When I eat you, you'll have to be quiet." She nodded and he watched her face as he slid his fingers into her sheath. "Ride my fingers, Rylee. Soak them so I can taste you on them."

"Nolan, I want to come." He told her to come and she moaned quietly through a climax. "It's not enough. I need you. I want to feel your cock in me. Your tongue in my pussy too."

Lifting the dress up so that it was around her hips, Nolan kissed her above her curls, then ran his tongue through her slit. She moaned again, her hips moving in a quick fucking imitation. Pulling her thighs apart, he sucked her clit into his mouth and bit down.

"Christ, yes." She came with her hand curled into his hair as her other hand was over her mouth. He sucked hard on her, bringing her again, and was rewarded with a mouth full of her hot juices. The more he ate of her, the more he drank from her until she begged him to stop.

Standing up, he opened his fly and freed his cock. Rylee wrapped her hand around him as she kissed him hungrily on the mouth. He loved the taste of her, and when she lapped at his mouth, tasting herself on him, he rocked into her hand as she fisted him. Working the zipper of her dress down in the back, he freed her breasts too and took one of them in his mouth.

"I want to come with you inside of me." Incapable of speaking, he moaned his approval. "Fuck me, Nolan, please. I need to feel you."

He lifted her up by her ass and rolled his cock round her heat until she begged him again. When he slid into her, slowly filling her as she begged him for more, all Nolan could think about was she was his. All his.

Fucking her this way, mindful of how quiet that they had to be, he leaned into her ear and bit down on her pretty lobe. When her pussy tightened around him, her teeth grazed over his neck and he moved so that she could have him. As soon as she told him she was coming, he held her mouth to his throat while she screamed, and he did as well when she sank her teeth deeply into his throat.

He came then, his body exploding into hers, his cock filling again almost as soon as he was empty. Fucking her harder now, glad for the wall behind him and not some flimsy piece of furniture, he marked her as well when the second, then third climax took him. Nolan saw stars dancing behind his lids as she screamed out her own release, holding his hand to her mouth.

Holding her upright was difficult. He was weak now, weaker than he'd ever been after sex, and wondered if they could stay here all night before anyone noticed they were gone. When his cellphone rang, he had to think how to answer it before she giggled and took it from him. As soon as he put it to his ear, he knew he was going to have to cut their evening short. It seemed that little Miss James was ready.

~~~

Rylee looked out over the woods behind their home and tried to think of something other than the fact that Shane wasn't home and that Walter had gone out as well. Nolan wasn't even due home for another couple of hours, having gone in to deliver a baby. Being alone wasn't all it was cracked up to be.

You could come into town and meet me after I'm finished here. She smiled when Nolan spoke to her. *Or, I could come home and find you naked in my bed waiting for me. Either one sounds good to me.*

I have to meet Constance at the mall in an hour. I don't want to be late. I have a feeling that she needs more from her dad than he realizes. He asked her what she meant. *I think she just left the house with nothing more than the clothes on her back. And Dennis isn't much better off. I feel badly for them.*

You should do some shopping as well. I have noticed that you're very low on panties. Something keeps happening to them. She told him it was all him, and that Reggie and Chris were going too. *They were going to go shopping anyway and had invited me to go. I'm not much of a shopper. I like online buying. Oh, and the first shipment of antiques came today. And the builders are saying that in two weeks we can move in. I think it will be quicker if Barron has anything to say about it. He's having a blast with this.*

She was too. Barron and Bentley Antiques was going to be huge. Not just in the building, all five floors of it, but in the amount of positive feedback they were getting. And Reggie had been helping her gather other things to put in the building as well. Homemade blankets and pottery. There was even a large jewelry case that had been in the things that were unearthed in the building they were going to put some of the finer pieces she'd been picking up. Day after tomorrow, she and Barron were going to an estate sale to see if they could get more of the smaller things they'd seen in the other shop they'd bought the entire inventory from just that morning.

I don't see how you can fail with him as your partner. His firsthand knowledge of things, as well as his expertise of wood, is going to make you a success. She thought so too. *Oh, before I forget to tell you, Walter has set up an appointment to get his GED. Then he wants to register for college next fall. And I think we might be looking into something on the horizon for Shane too. He has it in his head to follow after his dad.*

They had adopted both of them a week ago. The courts said it wasn't necessary for them to do so with Walter, as he was already an adult, but Shane said he wanted him as his brother legally. Nodding once, the judge signed the papers and now they had two sons. Shane still called her Aunt Rylee, but more and more he was calling her Mom. Nolan was just Dad, called that by both of the boys.

Alta is coming this weekend. She has some paperwork that Joey is taking care of for her, and I invited her to spend the weekend. Kason is coming as well. I think they're sweet on one another. Nolan though so too, he said. Rylee lay back on the grass and looked up at the sky. *I was also thinking about*

Christmas. I know it's a few months away, but what do you guys do for it? I'm betting you all get together at your mom's house.

We did last year, but it was decided that we'd share it from now on. Joey and Chris have it this year. You and I will next year, and whoever gets married over the next year, it will be theirs that year. She asked him if she thought the others would find their mates. *I do. I worry for Tony some, but I think he'll be all right. There are things that…he's been hurt, but none of us know for sure what it was.*

I think your grandda knows. He…he has a special feeling for Tony. Garth too. It could be that they're around him less with their own work, but he does love them. I love him too, the old fart. He laughed with her, and she looked up when a shadow fell over her face. *Well, I have to go I guess. Reggie is here and she's looking like she needs a break. Or she wants to go home with her babies.*

Both, I would imagine. I'm about done here anyway. The baby is doing fine after her struggle getting here, and both mom and daughter will be able to come home in a couple of days. Baby girl Donaldson had interrupted a nice game of chase between their cats when she'd decided that she wanted to come a couple of weeks early. It was the third baby he'd help bring into the world since the night of the charity event. *Burke is done with the hospital as of last night, and is going to be coming in all the time now. I, for one, am glad for it.*

As they made their way back to the house, Rylee realized just how lucky she was. A mate, a friend, and a family. Even a mother that she loved like her own, with grandparents that she could not get enough of. And now a business. This was what fairytales were made of, and she was glad to have gotten hers. Yes, Rylee thought, she was extremely lucky all the way around.

Now Available in the Bentley Legacy

Micah	Joseph	Nolan
Bentley Legacy Book 1	Bentley Legacy Book 2	Bentley Legacy Book 3

Before You Go...

HELP AN AUTHOR

write a review

THANK YOU!

Share your voice and help guide other readers to these wonderful books. Even if it's only a line or two your reviews help readers discover the author's books so they can continue creating stories that you'll love. Login to your favorite retailer and leave a review. Thank you.

AWARD WINNING, BESTSELLING AUTHOR

Kathi Barton, author of the bestselling series Force of Nature, lives in Nashport, Ohio with her husband Paul. In addition to writing full time Kathi likes to spend time with her eight grandkids, three children and three children-in-laws. She writes to relax and have fun.

Her muse, a cross between Jimmy Stewart and Hugh Jackman brings them to life for her readers in a way that has them coming back time and again for more. Her favorite genre is paranormal romance with a great deal of spice. You can visit Kathi on line and drop her an email if you'd like. She loves hearing from her fans. aaronskiss@gmail.com.

Follow Kathi on her blog:
http://kathisbartonauthor.blogspot.com/

www.ingramcontent.com/pod-product-compliance
Lightning Source LLC
Chambersburg PA
CBHW032128170626
46808CB00006B/2140

9781629893655